Geoff Tristram has been a prof[essional] over thirty-five years, working including Penguin, Embassy ..... Snooker, the BBC, Tarmac, Carillion, Past Times, Ravensburger Puzzles, Reeves, Winsor & Newton, Trivial Pursuit and the television show 'They Think It's All Over!', to name but a few. He has created artwork featuring the likes of Jonathan Ross, Jeremy Clarkson, Ian Botham, David Vine, Steve Bull, Alan Shearer and Ayrton Senna, not to mention virtually every famous snooker player that ever lifted a cue. You may even have noticed him at the Crucible World Championships on TV, interviewing the players as he drew their caricatures!

He has also illustrated many book covers, advertisements, album sleeves for bands such as UB40, The Maisonettes and City Boy (remember them?), and postage stamps, notably 'Charles and Diana – The Royal Wedding', 'Bermuda Miss World', 'Lake Placid Winter Olympics', and 'Spain 1982 World Cup Football'. More recently, his incredibly detailed 'Cat Conundrum', 'Best of British', and 'What If?' jigsaws have enthralled and exasperated thousands of dedicated puzzle fans all over the world.

Geoff's younger brother, David, is a well known and extremely successful comedy playwright and film-maker (check out the hilarious 'Doreen's Story', and the 'Inspector Drake' films on YouTube), so it was no real surprise when Geoff eventually turned his hand to comedy writing, hence this, his twelfth novel, 'The Last Cricket Tour'.

THE LAST CRICKET TOUR

Geoff Tristram

To Neil,
Best wishes,
Geoff Tristram

DRAWING
ROOM

The right of Geoff Tristram to be identified as author of this work has been asserted.

First published in 2014 by The Drawing Room Press.

Printed and bound by CPI Group (UK) Ltd, Croydon, CR0 4YY

ISBN 978-0-9926208-1-3

Edited by Copy Editor and Proofreader, Laura Tristram, MA (Publishing)

laura.anne.tristram@gmail.com – so blame her, not me.

Cover illustration by Geoff Tristram. Who else could I afford?

Buy books online at www.geofftristram.co.uk or contact the author on gt@geofftristram.co.uk

Dramatis Personae

Dennis Kensington – Club Secretary and Retired Accountant

Mike Wills – Chairman and Retired Brewery Manager

Barry Benfield – Cricket Coach and Van Driver

Paul and Amanda Beenie – Parents of Ben 'Beeno' Beenie

Ben 'Beeno' Beenie – Player and A-Level Student (All-Rounder)

Jay Taylor – Player and A-Level Student (Leg Spinner)

Ollie Henderson – Player and Primary School Teacher (Batsman)

Jeremy Lennox-Cameron – Player and Public Schoolboy (Batsman)

Dougie Lennox-Cameron – Jeremy's Father

Kevin Potts – Player and ex-Bank Manager (Batsman)

Gail Potts – Kevin Potts' Large Wife

Simon and Jacquie Grainger – Hotel Proprietors

Matt Wood – Player and Shakespeare Fan, First-Team Captain (Batsman)

Karen Perks – Matt's ex-Nurse Girlfriend

Gareth Evans – Welsh Overseas Player (Batsman)

Melanie Jones (Gareth's girlfriend)

Adam Trent – Player (Seam Bowler)

Shaun Lockwood – Player (Wicket Keeper)

Leo Jackman – Player (Bowler) and Wild Child

'Big' Jim Homer – Player (All-Rounder)

Sharon – A Prostitute

Cricket isn't life and death.
It's far more important than that!

Adapted from Bill Shankly's famous quote.

When sorrows come,
they come not single spies,
but in battalions.

William Shakespeare

Chapter 1

The Committee Meeting

'So that's it, is it?' asked Dennis. He sighed so heavily that his body appeared to be deflating at an alarming rate, like a punctured, withered old balloon.

''Fraid so,' said Barry resignedly, deflating a little himself in sympathy. 'We might as well throw the trowel in right now. It's no good sitting on the beach like King Lear, trying to stop the waves.'

'You mean towel, and it was King Canute actually, you bloody cretin,' interjected Mike. 'What school did you go to, if any? And remind me, what was it you came up with at the last meeting? If I recall, you were voting for Gail because she'd tickle your boxes...'

Dennis, who was well stricken in years, but looked even older, found enough energy to form a tired smile. Barry was a good friend, who, like himself, lived for the cricket club, but there was no denying the fact that he didn't possess the brightest intellect at Ashwood. He would often speak English as if it were his second or even third language, crunching his way through sentences with scant regard for correct grammar, tenses, pronunciation, or meaning, like a learner driver endeavouring to change gear during a twelve-point turn without employing the clutch.

'I have this golden rule when it comes to using expressions,' continued Mike, who didn't like to back off until he'd completely annihilated his opponents and ground them into the dust. 'Never bloody say anything unless you're sure you understand exactly what it *means*. Unless of course you actually intended to vote for Gail as Events Secretary because you liked the way she tickled your cricket box, perish the thought.'

'Okay, okay!' conceded Barry, colouring slightly. 'I didn't have the benefit of your bloody grammar school education, did I? Now can we wrap this up so I can bugger off home? There's something I wanted to see at half-eight.'

'Mastermind, was it?' asked Mike, sipping at his brandy and dry ginger, like a self-conscious student who'd just got an answer right on University Challenge.

'Go and bollocks!' said Barry, his stock response to virtually everything that in any way displeased him.

'Bollocks yourself. I shall never forget when you bought that second-hand laptop from Big Jim so you could record all the club statistics on it, and you asked me if you could use my UXB Mammary Stick.'

2

'Now now, girls,' chided Dennis, gradually inflating himself again, presumably by means of a hidden foot pump beneath the table. 'So – what options are left to us? Do we try to find another site for the club or simply give up and shut up shop after nearly a hundred years of proud history?'

'Well, I'm not sure it's a proud history exactly, but I'm with Barry on this,' admitted Mike, 'unlikely though that scenario must seem. My heart's not in relocating. Ashwood Cricket Club was founded here, on this very spot, in 1905, and has been here ever since. It wouldn't seem right being somewhere else, and besides that, we have to face facts. We're not exactly a thriving club are we? All the other clubs around here have at least two teams, and most have got three adult squads, a Sunday league team and several youth teams as well. We, on the other hand, can barely find enough people to turn out for the firsts. Jesus! We had a dog playing for us last Saturday.'

'He was a better fielder than most of us as well,' laughed Dennis. 'Did you see how he caught that one in the slips? It's a pity it took half of his teeth out. Poor thing must have been in agony after that.'

'It cost Matto nearly a hundred quid in vet's bills,' said Mike. 'He says Beefy isn't allowed to play with us anymore.'

'He isn't allowed to play with us anyway, I think you'll find,' replied Dennis, emptying half a bag of ready-salted nuts into his mouth and immediately wishing he hadn't. 'The opposithun capthin,' he continued, a tad sooner than he was able, 'got really stroppy about a dog being on the pitch. He complained to the umpires, but being as it was Norman and

3

Harry, who'd both played for Ashwood for forty-odd years before their hips went, it fell on deaf ears, both literally and metaphorically, as it were. They reckoned there was nothing in the rulebook to disallow it, but then their captain countered by saying the dog wasn't registered as a player and hadn't paid his subs, so it was illegal. It was all immaterial after it took the catch anyway, as it was rushed to the vets with blood all over its little face. Poor thing!'

'Well that proves my point,' continued Mike. 'We can't get a team most weeks. There's no youth coming through. They'd much rather play football or else get pissed on a Saturday – preferably both – and they're not too fussed about which order they do it in, some of them. Kids have got no attention span for cricket nowadays. The thought of standing around in a field all day is anathema to them.'

'What's an Affama?' asked Barry. 'I don't know that one.'

'A waste of good drinking time,' explained Mike, draining the last of his brandy with a mournful look, and signalling to the bored buxom barmaid for a replacement.

'I've dedicated my whole life to this place,' said Dennis, his eyes welling up suddenly. 'I can't bear to think that in a year's time it will be yet another hundred bloody apartments and a Tesco Express. What did that woman singer say once, the one who looked like a skull with long blonde hair? "You don't know what you've got till it's gone." Never was a truer word spoken, whoever she was.'

Dennis rose suddenly to visit the gents and Mike's gaze followed him out of the room. He was not sure if Dennis had

4

gone to relieve himself or secretly dab at his eyes with his hankie. Maybe it was to do both; a poor old club secretary simultaneously leaking at both ends. Mike and Barry sat in reverent silence until Dennis eventually returned, looking flushed, which was more than could be said for the decrepit changing room lavatory.

'So do we mark this sad occasion in some way or quietly crawl off home to be henpecked to death till we die of boredom?' asked Dennis, his voice breaking with emotion.

'We could have a big farewell dance or a buffet or something, I suppose,' suggested Barry, who liked his buffets and had a waistline and a pair of the *Daily Mail*'s special readers'-offer elasticated jogging bottoms to prove it.

'Yeah, a dance and a buffet, and we end up with eight folks, like last year,' said Mike, casting his colleague yet another withering glance.

'We should have one last hurrah!' Dennis said, with a sad, old lop-sided smile. 'Maybe a charity match against The Brickmaker's Arms Landlord's Eleven or whatever. They're the only ones we can beat nowadays.'

'Yes, we could do that, for sure,' agreed Barry, 'or – what about going on tour one last time, like we used to do when we were young?'

'Remember the Isle of Wight?' laughed Mike. 'Fat Brian got so pissed he woke up in Hastings covered in badly spelt tattoos and sporting a full beard. His missus never forgave him because he came home with the name Cheryl emblazoned on his back in six-inch capitals, and to this day, he hasn't got a clue how or why. He swears blind he's never even known anyone by the name of Cheryl, except that hard-faced bird from the Post Office, and she's a lesbian according to Kevin Potts, so it wasn't her.'

The three men, who weren't particularly given to raucous laughter, were now all but hysterical, with tears streaming down their cheeks. It was as if the mental image of Brian's flabby pink body, randomly covered in words hewn from a plethora of dodgy typefaces and married to a collection of naively drawn biological illustrations, had somehow shaved years off them, and they were suddenly carefree thirty-somethings once more. Had a passing psychiatrist observed the beneficial effects that this vivid memory seemed to be having on the trio, it would surely have only been a matter of time before he would start showing PowerPoint slides of similarly decorated fat folk to manic depressives as a form of therapy, and thereafter writing papers on the phenomenon, which he would of course name after himself.

'Go out with a bang, I say!' said Barry, wiping his watery eyes on his T-shirt. 'Let's go for it!'

'But could we get at least eleven folks interested?' queried Dennis. 'You said yourself we can hardly muster a full team for a home game some Saturdays.'

'Yes, true,' said Mike, 'but if we sell it big, as the last chance to play for the team, and we choose somewhere nice to play, maybe by the sea, I reckon we'll find enough folks.'

And so it was that Ashwood Cricket Club's selection committee decided unanimously to arrange a one-week tour in the summer. It proved to be a decision they would never forget.

Chapter 2

Four Months' Later

'Welcome to The Seaview Hotel,' said the tall, beaming, pinafore-clad gentleman who opened the front door. 'I presume you're the rest of our cricketers, judging by the kitbags. Come in, and I'll show you to your rooms.'

Paul and Mandy Beenie staggered over the threshold lugging their son Ben's kitbag behind them. It weighed just a little more than a narrowboat and stank to high heaven, largely, though not exclusively, because of a banana that Ben had left decomposing in there for three seasons, before it was discovered.

Mr Grainger, the hotel's proprietor, appeared to be wrestling with his emotions as the bag scudded past him and cannoned off his freshly painted skirting boards, its hopelessly inadequate wheels squealing and protesting under the weight. Ben Beenie, a seriously talented, if cocky, little sixteen-year-old who looked far more like the Milky Bar Kid than, say, a young Ian Botham, strode in behind them, gazing this way and that with snake eyes, as he did when he arrived at the crease and was memorizing potential weaknesses in the field placings, prior to hammering his first six out of the ground. Behind him came Jay Taylor, his friend, only seventeen, but already a foot taller and five years more hirsute than his team mate. Jay was the lazy labrador to Ben Beenie's nippy terrier. He too would have been a decent player had he not been born the most laid-back youth in Christendom. Behind Jay Taylor came Jay Taylor's equally huge kitbag, which – if kitbags are capable of thought – was hell-bent on demolishing the Seaview reception area out of sheer malice, just because it could. Once Mr Grainger had restored his picture frames, his vase of artificial flowers and the RSPCA charity box to their rightful places, and then swept up the items that sadly didn't make it, he took a deep breath and announced that he would show the lads to their shared room first, if the adults would be so kind as to remain where they were and resist the temptation to tear his new Dralon curtains down. This they dutifully did, for five minutes or so, until Mr Grainger strode back through the dining room to join them. The three then made their way up the creaky stairs, and it was at around the eighth step that Paul Beanie's mobile began to ring. He excused himself and dug the phone out from his trouser pocket, clicked the green button and raised the instrument to his ear.

'We're down the pub,' said his son Ben – Beeno to his friends.

'What?' queried Paul Beenie. 'What do you mean, you're down the pub? You're in your room.'

'We dumped the stuff and then Jay's mobile rang. It was Ollie. He said the rest of the lads were down the pub at the end of the street so we're there now. Come down when you've unpacked if you like, as long as you don't embarrass me.'

'But how did you get there so quickly? We only left you a minute ago?' asked Paul, nonplussed.

'Window in our room was open so me and Jay hopped through it. Oh, hang on, gotta go. Jay's playing pool with a prostitute.'

And with that, Beeno hung up.

'We have been in Pitbank-on-Sea for precisely five minutes,' announced Paul Beenie, looking and sounding somewhat shell-shocked, 'and the boy that we have been asked to look after for the week is playing pool with a prostitute.'

'Ah, that'll be The Crown just down the road,' chipped in Mr Grainger. 'We do get a lot of them go in there I'm afraid. Prostitutes I mean, not cricketers. Never mind. At least he's only playing pool with one, and not, you know, the other thing. Shall I show you to your room then?'

'You better had,' groaned Paul Beenie. 'We need to get down there now, before they start having sex on the pool table while the others goad him on, like a scene from one of those Southern States hillbilly films starring Burt Reynolds, and erm, what's-her-name.'

'Jodie Foster?' suggested Mr Grainger helpfully. Mr Beenie shrugged non-committally.

Mandy Beenie said nothing – at least, not with her mouth, which was set in an open position, rather like that of a halibut that had been whacked across the brow with a fisherman's priest without prior written warning. However, even without the gift of speech, she was still managing to convey a message to her husband along the lines of, *What the HELL are we doing in this God-forsaken dump when we were offered seven days in the sun at my parents' villa in the Costa Blanca, free of charge?*

Paul Beenie flashed her a desperate look, and then, with admirable composure, he began chatting to his host about the test-match highlights, as they opened the hotel-room door. He was greeted by the usual Bed and Breakfast Decor Disaster. Vivid pink and tangerine vertical stripes, huge floral wallpaper borders with chipped and peeling edges, utility wardrobe, ghastly, dusky-pink Dralon quilted headboard, tatty black television mounted on the wall by means of an ugly extending bracket, an en suite in violently clashing avocado; nasty, battered, teak coffee table replete with small plastic furred-up kettle, two shortbread biscuits, four UHT milks and a 'What's On in Devon' leaflet that should really have been subtitled 'Not Much'.

'Everything okay with your room?' asked Mr Grainger.

'Lovely, thanks!' replied Mr and Mrs Beenie, in sickly sweet two-part harmony.

11

'We'd better unpack later and get down the pub then,' added Paul Beenie, loosening his collar after negotiating what seemed like an Everest of steep steps without a Sherpa to carry the luggage. A small bead of sweat rolled down his brow, and landed on the pink nylon duvet.

The Crown was heaving. Paul and Mandy Beenie pushed their way through the crowded lounge to the TV-room-cum-sports-bar at the back of the pub, where the pool table was situated. The Ashwood lads greeted the Beenies and raised their glasses to them. Most looked as if they were on their third or fourth pint, judging by their ruddy complexions and the volume of their voices. In the centre of the room, a stunned-looking Jay Taylor was chalking his tip distractedly. A heavily tattooed, scantily clad, skinny woman in her mid-forties stood behind him, feeling his buttocks. Jay Taylor's imploring look said it all. It said, 'please, Mr and Mrs Beenie, would you please, please get me out of here, NOW!'

Behind the two pool players, Beeno looked on, smirking.

'Jay!' shouted Paul Beenie, from the far end of the sports bar. 'Er, come on, mate, we need to get going.' Jay made his excuses to the woman and sidled off in the direction of his saviours. Ollie placed his fifty-pence piece on the cush to book the next game.

'I charge more than that, you cheeky fucker,' cackled the woman, her Joe Cocker vocal tone presumably the result of a cigarette habit that she had probably enjoyed since early

12

childhood. Ollie retrieved his cash and backed away nervously.

'Jeez!' said Jay Taylor, heading for the exit with his guardians. 'You won't believe what she just asked me to do to her in the ladies' loos.'

'Beeno!' hissed his mother. 'You need to come too, we're going.'

'I'm on next,' explained Beeno. 'I'll be out in a bit.'

'You'll be out now!' she snarled, and Beeno got the message this time. He slouched across the floor with a look that said, 'It's not fair.' It was hard to judge whether he was complaining about losing his fifty-pence piece or not losing his virginity.

Rather than waste a turn at the pool table, Club Treasurer, Kevin Potts, stepped in to spend his young star batsman's hard-earned cash for him. Kevin was a fifty-five-year-old ex-bank manager who had probably been quite a handsome fellow in his younger days, and was still a fit-looking individual, if one discounted the formative beer belly. He was covered from head to toe in thick, dark hair, with a solitary three-inch shaved gap between the nape of his neck and his back. It was as if miniature explorers had carved a clearing through dense tropical rainforest so that they could build a road. Kevin was the sort who had to shave his entire face each morning, being careful to avoid the eyebrows.

The prostitute eyed him up and down as a mongoose would scrutinize its breakfast snake, and in typically fickle fashion, as befits a dedicated sex worker, moved in on her hirsute new pool partner, with Jay Taylor now nothing more than a vague and distant memory. Not wishing to look too forward or cheap, her opening gambit involved rubbing the crotch of Kevin's jeans in a slow, rhythmic way, in order to concentrate his mind, or possibly even to put him off his break, whilst mouthing quiet obscenities. Meanwhile, his fat, surly wife, Gail, sat in the sunshine outside nursing a sweet sherry and chatting to elder statesmen Mike, Barry and Dennis. Sipping occasionally at her drink and enjoying the sunshine, she was blissfully unaware of what was going on in the sports bar. It was just as Mr and Mrs Beenie, their son Beeno and their adopted teenager for the week, Jay Taylor, joined them, that the outdoor party noticed a rather burly-looking woman with curly, unkempt, shoulder-length hair heading down the street in their direction.

'Bloody hell!' said Barry, lowering his glass from his lips in disgust. 'If this is typical of the Pitbank-on-Sea females, I think I'm catching the next bus to Torquay. Jeeeezus!'

The burly woman, who had legs like a rugby player's and was just about wearing a garish flower-pattern mini dress, swigged cider from a can, and had just emitted an odious burp that could be heard as far away as Cornwall, providing the wind was in the right direction – or perhaps the wrong direction, if one sees it from the Cornish perspective. As she neared the dumbstruck group huddled on the pub benches outside The Crown, she lifted her dress to reveal a pair of off-white underpants that featured, quite bizarrely, a picture of Cliff Richard that had been rather badly distorted by the contents of the underwear, causing our foremost Christian vocalist to bear a most unfortunate resemblance to Joseph Merrick, a.k.a. the Elephant Man. Either the woman had recently shoplifted a banana and two oranges and chosen to smuggle them out of Sainsbury's in her underwear, or else she was a transvestite.

'Greetings everybody!' grinned Shaun, the wicket keeper – for it was he. His face appeared to have been made-up by a talented chimpanzee, with bright red lipstick at least half an inch wider than the contours of his lips. His vivid eye shadow looked as if the chimpanzee had simply thrown two small pots of Kingfisher Blue paint at him from a few yards away. If that was what had actually happened, then, all things considered, it wasn't a bad job. However, the twenty-year-old's immature beard did somewhat spoil the overall effect, if an effect so awful in the first place could indeed be further spoiled. Worryingly, none of this seemed to be putting off the two drunks who walked past at that juncture with bags of chips, one of whom (the men, not the chips) was heard to slur the words, '...and any port in a storm, I say!' to his inebriated companion.

Dennis, being in his seventies, had forgotten what it was like to be young and crazy and on tour, if one excludes the brief trip down memory lane at the committee meeting four months' previously, sparked by talk of Fat Brian's tattoo collection. He merely gave Shaun a withering look and asked what he'd come as.

'Ah!' said Shaun, lobbing his empty can at the waste bin and missing by a mile, which was not what one wanted to see from a first-team wicket keeper. 'It was Gareth's idea, our new overseas player.'

'Wales is not, to my knowledge, overseas,' said Mike dryly.

'Whatever,' said Shaun, with a dismissive wave of the hand. He burped again, this time with enough force to cause structural damage to nearby buildings. 'Gareth found a couple of his sister's old dresses in the charity bag, so he's brought them on tour as a forfeit. The players are going to vote on who's been the biggest twat of the day, and whoever it is has to wear the dress that evening, no matter where we go. We've got a spare pink one as well in my kitbag, so at least they'll get a choice.'

'And why are *you* wearing it?' asked Mike, who possessed an enquiring mind and an insatiable thirst for knowledge.

'Ah! Because I was map reader on the trip down here and we ended up in a trading estate the other side of Stoke-on-Trent.'

'I see. Well, easily done, in fairness. The two places have similar characteristics. Anyway, the dress suits you, I think.'

'Thank you. So that's why we're late arriving. Anyway, Gareth and the other two are just unpacking, so I'm off inside to watch the test match on the telly. See you at the dinner tonight!'

And with that, he flounced inside. It was worth going back into the pub, Jay suggested, just to see how Shaun and the prostitute got on. His bet was that Shaun would almost certainly be more successful, vis-à-vis rough trade, than the lady at the pool table had been.

Had Jay Taylor been tempted to have a flutter at the town's Ladbrokes, based on his instinct, he would in fact have lost his money. The Prostitute (let's call her Sharon for the sake of brevity, it being two syllables fewer than 'The Prostitute') was currently in the less than salubrious ladies' lavatory. She had booked a private cubicle and was sharing this Spartan, cramped, Dettol-scented water closet with Kevin Potts, who had parted with some of his spending money after much haggling, in return for fellatio and whatever else Sharon could recommend from her huge and exotic repertoire.

It was at this precise and unfortunate juncture that Mrs Gail Potts, the sturdy, dour wife of Kevin Potts, chose to empty her bladder after finally emptying her sherry glass. At first, she suspected that there must be a woman in the cubicle who had dashed in there in order to give birth prematurely, judging by the grunts and groans that were emanating from under the door of Cubicle 3. She was about to summon help from within the pub, when she instead decided to crouch down – not an easy task when one is built like Mrs Potts – and look under the lavatory door. Imagine her displeasure when she realized that her knees were now sat in a puddle of freezing cold water, and then her astonishment when she spied not two feet, but four, and *then* imagine what was going through her mind when she duly observed that one of the pairs of feet was wearing the rather smart Grenson brogues that she had bought her husband for his fifty-fifth birthday. This, of course, could have been a coincidence. No doubt there were hundreds of men wearing identical shoes to Kevin's at that precise moment, scattered around the country. However, it was at this pivotal stage of Mrs Potts' deliberations, when the benefit of the doubt was still a plausible option, that the disembodied voice of Kevin Potts wailed, 'Oh God! Ha ha ha ha hooooo! Jesus!', and in an instant, Gail had made a judgment and knew what had to be done. With a face even more like thunder than usual, she strode to the sink and began filling a carrier bag, which she always kept in her handbag for emergencies, with cold tap water. She would have preferred boiling hot, but sadly it was taking too long to arrive. Meanwhile, inside the cubicle, all had gone quiet, as Kevin's post-coital *petit mort* set in. Gail launched the swollen water bomb over the top of the cubicle with admirable technique, and immediately its effects were felt by those within. Amid much swearing and screaming, the lavatory door burst open, with a livid Kevin Potts willing and able to tear the perpetrator into small pieces. Gail stood in front of the door, meaty arms set like the handles on an obese cricket cup, fists glued to her ample sides, her bulk casting a dark shadow and blotting out the light from the hammered-glass window behind her.

Kevin had, in his time, faced many a ferocious bowler, but this was nothing compared to what he had to face now. Behind him, a soaking wet Sharon, hair like rats' tails, scowled and tried in vain to light a damp cigarette.

'Who's this fat ugly cow?' she asked.

Kevin seemed to have lost the power of speech. A split second later, the full force of Gail's massive handbag – laden with his and her car keys, the two hotel-room keys (each attached to sizeable sheets of red, numbered Formica), an industrial-sized make-up bag, a purse full-to-bursting with half a ton of loose change, and two spectacle cases – caught him a purler on the bridge of his nose, rendering him temporarily senseless. Kevin staggered backwards, demolishing the bag of skin and bones that was Sharon, who fell back into the open-lidded lavatory bowl, jack-knifing and sinking so deeply into the abyss that her buttocks became submerged in the unspeakable, yellow water below.

Gail, her job done, turned on her heels in the manner made famous by Miss Piggy, and exited the lavatory block like an Olympic Power Walker, heading for the NCP car park and pursued unsteadily by her addled husband.

And then, they were ten.

That evening, the dinner, at the nearby 'Family-Friendly Fun Pub', The Pirate and Parrot, was a raucous affair, at least down the younger end of the Last Supper-sized trestle table next to Captain Jack's Jungle Room. However, at the elderly end, two poignant, empty seats served as a graphic reminder to all gathered there, that if men are not fed well at home, they are prone to eat out; often at cheap takeaways. Even more importantly, it also reminded members of the Ashwood Cricket Club that they were now one man down, with their first game scheduled for 1pm the following day. The good news was that Leo Jackman, who couldn't make the trip on Monday due to mysterious 'commitments', was supposed to be arriving just in time for the game on Tuesday. Those who knew 'Jackass' well, were not holding their breath.

Dinner concluded, the Elder Statesmen, led by Dennis, resplendent in a fetching baby-blue cable-knit pullover with little leather cricket-ball buttons, knitted especially for the tour by his wife, Doris, retired to the Seaview bar for a quiet brandy and bed, whilst the younger element headed for the bars and nightclubs. The two lads not yet old enough to drink alcohol, Jay Taylor and Beeno, were headed off at the pass by Mr and Mrs Beenie and shepherded back to their room – with great reluctance – to watch television, their phoney I.D. cards confiscated.

It is fair to say that the boys felt very hard done to, and accordingly their mood was subdued, entirely due to the interference of Beeno's 'overly fussy' parents, who had faithfully sworn not to embarrass the lad in front of his peers, in return for being allowed to join him on tour and also finance it. Little did the two young cricketers know, as they sat stony-faced, Cokes in hand, watching a repeat of 'Come Dine with Me', what adventures lay in store for them, later that same evening.

Chapter 3

The Full English

The breakfast room of the Seaview Hotel was only sparsely populated at 8.30am, and those who had made it seemed to be the non-playing members of the touring party; namely Dennis, Mike, Barry and Mr and Mrs Beenie, who looked ashen. Those fully cognizant of the facts would not find this poor turnout surprising.

After parting company with the Elder Statesmen and the Underage Two, the cricketers descended on a bar at the end of the pier, as would a swarm of locusts. These were not your typical locusts, however – the sort that tend to prefer grain crops, vegetables and the like, leaving an area barren and starving in their wake. The Ashwood locust, a sub-species, was more interested in stripping a town of its alcohol, so that future visitors were left with absolutely nothing to drink, other than tea, coffee and fizzy pop. It is fair to say that Pierre's Pier Bar, a vaguely French-themed tourist establishment, didn't know what had hit it. Once those lads of dubious vintage had persuaded the burly bouncer that their I.D. cards were kosher – proof that they were old enough to destroy their remaining brain cells with copious amounts and varieties of alcohol if they so wished – the touring party dashed for the bar as would contestants on Supermarket Sweep, desperate to begin the delirium process.

For the sake of clarity, it needs to be explained that Beeno and Jay Taylor were not the only underage lads on tour. Jeremy Lennox-Cameron was a mere, peach-cheeked stripling of fifteen, but he was among those present largely due to the fact that his father, Dougie, wasn't arriving until the following day, and what dad didn't know wouldn't hurt him. This, as one could readily imagine, had not gone down at all well with Messers Taylor and Beeno, who were currently under house arrest in spite of both being older than young Jeremy.

Smuggling the baby-faced Beeno into a club or bar would have called for considerable initiative, but Jeremy was an even more challenging case. He did not look even *close* to eighteen. In fact, he barely looked fourteen, thanks to his choirboy features and complete lack of facial hair, a dilemma that was eating away at Matto, the first-team captain. (For some strange reason – probably complete lack of imagination – many of the players at Ashwood were inevitably given a nickname that ended with the letter O.)

After considerable thought, Matto decided that the best solution was to borrow his girlfriend Karen's smoky eye shadow, and create for young Jeremy a five o'clock shadow effect. In the dark, at the end of the pier, this just about looked passable, if everyone half closed their eyes and squinted at the lad, but this alone did nothing to improve his voice tone, which owed more to Aled Jones in his Snowman days than, say, Clint Eastwood. The best advice, offered by Ollie, was to keep his head down and grunt, 'Okay mate?' at the bouncer with as deep a voice as he could muster, when the time came. As a back-up, Gareth, the overseas player, would slip his own I.D. card to Jeremy once he'd been allowed into the bar, by means of some clever sleight of hand and distraction techniques, learnt in the seedier areas of Cardiff on numerous Saturday nights, when he was an underage A-Level student.

First at the door was wicket keeper Shaun, still resplendent in his floral dress and make-up. Wrongly or rightly, the other lads had theorized that, if the burly bouncer would let this exotic creature in, then surely all else would follow, as night follows day. They needn't have worried in that regard. Not only did the bouncer let his first transvestite of the week past the rope, he even added words of encouragement, the precise nature of which went unheard by the rest of the queuing cricketers. Next up came a succession of bona-fide candidates who obviously must have looked their age, even if they didn't act it, and then, slipped in strategically at number six, as befitted a middle order batsman, was Jeremy Lennox-Cameron, cherubic public schoolboy and alcohol virgin. A huge tattooed hand barred his way.

'How old are you?' asked its owner gruffly in a marked West Country burr.

'Erm, nineteen,' growled Jeremy, staring at his feet. The affected vocal style that he fondly imagined was akin to Lee Marvin's, in reality sounded as if he were practising his end of term ventriloquism act, but without the dummy. The voice seemed to be coming from somewhere down the back of his throat. Gareth, who had just been let through by the bouncer, now tapped the man on the back, desirous of a word.

'Oh, excuse me,' he began in his strong, Welsh brogue, smiling sweetly at the man mountain. 'The thing of it is, as it happens, old Jerry here is actually nineteen, look you, but we calls him Baby Face, see, on account of—'

'I.D.' demanded the bouncer.

Luckily, during Gareth's subterfuge, he had managed to flick his I.D. card behind the bouncer's back, to be expertly caught by Jeremy. A lesser mortal might have found the spinning sheet of plastic-encapsulated card impossible to catch, but Matto's insistence on rigorous weekly fielding work-outs had reaped dividends. As if from nowhere, Jeremy produced the I.D. card and flashed it at the man, albeit briefly. The bouncer coughed sarcastically and, without uttering a single word, managed to convey the impression that he wanted to examine it at close quarters. Jeremy resignedly handed it over.

'This feller here,' he said, pointing the finger of suspicion at the public schoolboy with the smoky-grey beard, 'has got a mop of almost black, Beatle-like hair, and the chap on this card has got proper blond, spiky hair, more akin to early David Bowie.'

This bouncer knew his rock-star hairdos alright. Jeremy's already rosy cheeks got considerably rosier.

'In fact,' continued the bouncer, warming to his theme, 'this blond bugger is you, you bloody Welsh twat.'

'I'm sure that was racist,' complained Gareth.

'It was,' confirmed the bouncer, helpfully.

Matto, observing that things were not going as smoothly as he would have liked, strode back to the queue to see if he could pour oil on troubled waters.

'Can I have a quick word?' he asked the bouncer. The bouncer begrudgingly accommodated him, adding that he hadn't got all night. Matt drew him to one side and whispered in his ear, at length. The bouncer then seemed to be weighing heavy things in his mind, and, once he'd made his decision, he reluctantly opened the rope and allowed Jeremy inside, followed by the remaining Ashwood squad members.

Once inside the bar, the team gathered round, eager to see how their captain had pulled off what they considered to be a minor miracle.

'Oh, well I knew Jerry stood no chance, so I told the chap that we had two transgender players in the team, who we'd taken on in order to get extra funding from the lottery: Shaun he'd already met, who had begun living as a female only this week, which explains why he's so crap at it, and Jemima, who is going through the process of travelling in the opposite direction, as it were, and was soon to become a full-time bloke. I explained that the painted-on beard was just her way of trying to look more manly, and she was currently working on the voice, which was still very much female. I also mentioned that her age wasn't an issue, because she was in fact twenty-six, but she was loathe to show her I.D. because it pictured her as the woman she once was, if you follow me. I asked if he'd just quietly let her through to avoid drawing attention to her at a time when she was feeling extremely vulnerable.'

'Fuck me!' said Ollie. 'You are a fucking genius, skipper. I can see now why the selection committee chose you to lead us in battle!'

Jeremy, too, looked on in wonder, though in his case his admiration for the captain was tainted by the several mixed emotions that were currently rattling about in his head. Emotions that resurfaced not long after, when a much-mellowed bouncer offered to buy him a glass of wine and show him around the town when his shift was over. Shaun, too, seemed to have found a persistent admirer, who was either seriously myopic, or sexually weird, or both. Eventually, he had to be firm, and tell the drunken fellow that he wasn't that kind of girl (or any kind of girl, for that matter). When that didn't work either, he simply threatened to 'beat the living shit' out of him, a threat he was more than capable of carrying out.

By 2am, the team was seriously the worse for wear. Gareth was trying to play on the one-armed bandit, but was so inebriated that he was just pulling the handle and laughing hysterically to himself. As the bouncer strode past him to investigate a commotion at the far end of the pub, the Welshman grabbed hold of his beefy arm and pointed out a huge pile of vomit, just to the left of the slot machine.

'I just puked down there, mate,' he explained. 'Can you get it up for me?'

Seconds later, Gareth was lying on the planked floor of the pier, with absolutely no recollection of how he'd ended up there. His right ear, he quickly realized, was throbbing horribly, and it was only a matter of time, he believed, before his stomach exploded. Then, one by one, his team mates joined him, in various degrees of mental and physical decay. Some had left the bar of their own volition, having witnessed the ejection of their Welsh International. Others, like Ollie, had been asked to leave after he tried to separate two lesbians in the middle of a long, lingering kiss, in order that he could be allowed to have a go. Worst affected by far was young Jeremy, who had never tasted alcohol before, and was looking sicker than a landlubber on an R.N.L.I. lifeboat in a gale-force-nine hurricane just off the Shetland Islands.

Somehow, this motley crew found its way back to the Seaview Hotel (via several wrong turns and a pensioner's garden), where the older members and the two players under house arrest were tucked up in bed and fast asleep. It was at this juncture that Gareth's Doctor Jekyll persona suddenly and inexplicably gave way to his alter ego, Mr Hyde. Without any prior warning, Gareth removed all of his clothing as he stood in the breakfast room. Followed by several other curious players, he made his way to Jay Taylor and Beeno's shared room, and found Beeno's kitbag parked outside. He opened the bag and rummaged drunkenly, throwing the contents hither and thither, until he found what he'd presumably been looking for. Or maybe not – it was impossible to tell. He whipped out a bright-pink bat grip, and for the uninitiated, this is a tube of dimpled rubber that fits tightly over the handle of the bat to aid secure, non-slip handling. He then attached it to his penis, as one would a condom, and was delighted and not a little proud to see that it stayed on, and fitted him like a glove – an incredibly unsuitable expression if one is forced to think about it. Next, Gareth tried the bedroom door, and to his further delight, found that it was unlocked. He charged into the room with a blood-curdling scream that would have woken those in hospital-induced comas, putting the fear of God into Beeno and Jay Taylor, who had been dreaming peacefully about knocking a double century at Lord's and making love to a nubile young lady named Lauren, respectively. Gareth grabbed a groggy Jay by his feet and yanked him to the edge of the bed, where he began to simulate coarse anal sex whilst yelling at the top of his voice, 'Come on Jay, you want me don't you, you know you do!'

All this was observed by a terrified Beeno, and a growing band of nonplussed players who had just arrived. Captain Matt, who liked horseplay as much as the next man, did nevertheless question the wisdom of appointing Gareth as his Child Protection Officer, if this was the kind of thing he got up to once he'd had a few drinks. Maybe, he pondered, he should discreetly bring this up at the next committee meeting, and they could vote in Ollie instead, being as he was a junior school teacher and had to be regularly CRB checked. He may have had a secret penchant for lesbians when he'd had a couple, but with young lads he was completely sound.

While all this was happening downstairs, Jeremy was staggering up around forty flights of stairs, trying to find his bed, and leaving little puddles of vomit as markers, should he need to retrace his steps at any point. It was when he began to sob brokenly that he came to the attention of Mr and Mrs Beenie.

Paul Beenie, who had slept but fitfully, was on his way to the bathroom to relieve himself in the ghastly avocado lavatory, when he heard strange noises coming from just outside his room. He doubled back and opened the bedroom door to find a bedraggled, foul-smelling, chubby youth projectile vomiting all over the hallway carpet – not what you want at three in the morning, or any other time, for that matter.

'What on earth is up?' he asked.

'I'm being sick,' explained Jeremy helpfully, in between being sick.

'Well can't you do it in the sink in your room?' asked Paul, studying the myriad pools of vomit with dismay. 'When Mr Grainger sees this lot, he'll probably throw us all out first thing in the morning. Bloody hell!'

'C-C-Can't find my room,' said Jeremy, before heaving again and depositing a sizeable amount of yellowish-green fluid onto Paul Beenie's new M&S slippers.

'What number is it?' asked Beeno's dad, who wasn't the strongest stomached of folk himself. He removed the slippers gingerly, so that his wife could clean them for him in the morning.

'Dunno,' sobbed Jeremy, who had always reminded Paul Beenie of Eeyore, the lovable depressed donkey from the

Winnie the Pooh stories. Seeing him drunk and vomiting at three in the morning, however, had rather put paid to that cosy image, and now all he wanted to do was hit him in the face with a shovel and put the little shit out of his misery. Resisting the desire to sift through his luggage for a suitable blunt instrument, Paul began to gingerly frisk the sodden corpse, and found that there was a hard, six-inch-long object lurking in Jeremy's trousers. To his immense relief, this turned out to be the Perspex key fob, bearing the legend 'Room 20', the room directly opposite Paul's, joy of joys. Paul placed the lad against a wall to try to prevent him from falling over, and opened the door to Jeremy's room. Inside, an open suitcase was sitting in the middle of the floor, and judging by its surroundings, it appeared that terrorists had planted a bomb inside it. There were items of clothing everywhere, toiletries strewn across the bed, cricket magazines, cans of pop, and all manner of medications. Paul returned to the corridor to find Jeremy was now horizontal. He scooped him up, desperately trying to avoid any damp bits, and shovelled him into the bedroom and onto the bed, where Jeremy promptly threw up again, all over the pink nylon duvet. Paul stared at the wall for a full minute, as his fevered brain ran the gamut of emotions from A to Z and then back again. It was at this point that he heard what sounded like ten tons of coal being deposited into an unseen coal cellar. Spinning around to see what had caused the commotion, he was greeted by a naked Welshman with a giant fluorescent penis, which he was swinging around like the propeller of a four-seater Cessna aircraft.

'Weeeeeey!' said the Welshman.

Behind him, three or four similarly naked individuals – Paul was too weary to count them accurately – shouted back 'Weeeeeeey!' in response. Gareth's girlfriend, Melanie, usually a shy and retiring young lady, was also stark naked, and was sporting a pair of large gold tassels on her fulsome breasts, in the style made popular by Turkish belly dancers.

'Jesus Christ!' hissed Paul Beenie, 'Can you lot be quiet? You're going to get us all kicked out of this place before we've even played a single game of cricket!'

'Weeeeeeeeeey!' came the response, and just behind an exhausted Paul Beenie came the sound of a young public schoolboy vomiting again. Realizing that any form of rational conversation was utterly pointless, Paul pushed past the naked revellers and shut himself in his room, locking the door after him. Outside, the screams and banging noises headed off, presumably down the stairs, until they became dull thuds and distant raised voices at the other end of the large, rambling hotel.

Mrs Amanda Beenie, hiding in her bed and fearing for her life, demanded to know what was going on.

'What's going on,' explained Paul Beenie, is we're going home first thing in the morning.'

The next thing he knew, it *was* morning, and a glorious one at that. Seagulls were squawking just outside the window, as they are prone to doing in seaside towns or on inland council tips. Other than this, all was still, and all that was needed to complete this unexpected scene of tranquillity was a backing track of Edvard Grieg's Peer Gynt Suite No. 1. Maybe it was

31

because the morning was, so far at least, a most welcome polar opposite of the previous evening, that Paul Beenie had mellowed a little vis-à-vis his threat to return home, or maybe it was the smell of the full English breakfasts being prepared downstairs. Whatever the reason, he quickly showered and shaved, and his wife did likewise but in different places, and ten minutes later, marginally refreshed but still looking somewhat grey from the previous evening's shenanigans, the Beenies entered the breakfast room to find, as has already been mentioned, a team of cricketers noticeable only by their absence.

Mr Grainger entered, wearing his pinny and took orders for tea and coffee. Paul Beenie nervously examined the proprietor's drawn-looking features and erroneously presumed that he had witnessed at least some of the antics of the Ashwood Cricket Team, and was about to launch into his reasons for booting out the entire squad once they'd had breakfast. Further probing revealed that the Graingers had not heard a thing, due to the fact that their private quarters were tucked away in some far-flung outpost of the rambling hotel. World War Three could have broken out, he explained, and they wouldn't have known about it. Paul Beenie breathed a sigh of relief, but tempered his feelings by reminding himself that some poor unfortunate Albanian chambermaid would any time soon be discovering the delights of the south wing – namely Jeremy Lennox-Cameron's room and the fifty piles of rank vomit that would lead her there.

It transpired that Mr Grainger was looking drawn that morning because, immediately after breakfast, he and his tearful wife would have to make their way to his mother-in-law's funeral. Paul and Amanda Beenie looked at each other in horror. What the Graingers really needed at that point was a rampaging horde of rapers and pillagers that would make Attila the Hun look like Gloria Hunniford.

Shortly after this bombshell had gone off, players began to file into the breakfast room in ones and twos, and most were complaining about their dreadful hangovers and clutching at passing walls for support. Noticeable by his absence was one Jeremy Lennox-Cameron, who had presumably ejected his stomach and most of his intestines in the night, and was therefore physically, as well as psychologically, unable to enjoy breakfast, or any other meal, ever again.

Jay Taylor and Beeno sat with the Beenies and ordered everything on the menu. Mr Beenie's enquiry about how their night in had gone was met with awkward silence and hasty sideways glances aimed at the table where a decidedly green-looking Gareth was sitting with his matching green girlfriend. Paul Beenie looked over as casually as he could, but had no idea at that stage that the lads had also been subjected to a close encounter with the pink bat grip. He nodded briefly at the sheepish Welshman, who nodded back before burying his head in his cornflakes. Paul then focussed his gaze on the large bay window behind Gareth that boasted a panoramic view of the sea, and observed that the two giant, gold, Dralon curtains that framed the view seemed to be missing their ornamental tassels. All that remained was a crudely frayed bit of gold string. He gulped audibly and then went off searching for cereal to take his mind off things.

Dennis Kensington, now resplendent in a green cable-knit pullover, sat buttering his toast, also seemingly oblivious to the night-time chaos his beloved cricket club had inflicted on a grieving couple. He did, however, warn the assembled group that drinking to excess the night before an important game was foolhardy. It was one thing to be hung-over and idling around the shops and on the pleasure beach, but quite another to be hung-over and required to play a full day's cricket. Maybe because the missing player was of his own peer group and not one of the youngsters, he omitted to add that it was also irresponsible to end up in a lavatory with a prostitute the day before a game. Kevin Potts' rush of blood to the privates had caused a major headache for the team. Now they were reliant on Leo Jackman turning up on time – not something he was renowned for – in order to prevent them from fielding a weakened side. Not only that, Dennis continued, they now had no contingency plan if another player became injured, or succumbed to alcohol poisoning. Obviously, no one had yet had the nerve to bring up the subject of young Jeremy.

An hour later, and breakfast concluded, the players retired to their rooms to take paracetamol and cold showers, gather their belongings and meet outside the hotel, ready to travel in convoy ten miles down the road to Pebbleton Bay Cricket Club.

After a brief medical examination by Barry the coach, Jeremy Lennox-Cameron was deemed unfit for cricket, or indeed for anything, and was left in his room to recuperate, or if not, quietly decease. That would have meant the Ashwood team was reduced to just nine men, but thankfully, Jeremy's father, Dougie, was en route to the Pebbleton ground to join the tour party and watch his son play, so he would have to replace his wilting offspring, just for one day. Barry had gathered together Jeremy's kit and was taking it to the ground for Jeremy's father to wear, in spite of the fact that his son was conservatively a foot shorter than he was and had a waist half the size. Dougie was not the most tactical of cricketers, and he would never seen fifty again, but what he lacked in skill, he made up for with enthusiasm, and besides, beggars couldn't be choosers. He would have to do.

Now all they needed was to hold their splitting heads together and somehow concentrate for a whole afternoon. Oh yes, and they also needed to hope and pray that the right Leo Jackman turned up. There were two, you see, and no one was ever quite sure which one they'd get.

Chapter 4

A Spectacular Entrance and departure from Jackass

Pebbleton Cricket Club was a pretty little place. It had a banked, grassy area around the pitch, which gave it the look of a Roman amphitheatre. To one side there was a nice view of the sea, and on the opposite side was a canal, where people could promenade on sunny days, and maybe eat a picnic on the many waterside benches provided by the local council. Behind the canal was a track on which old-style steam railway engines chuffed up and down, tooting to the boat owners and cricketers as they passed by. Swans hissed aggressively at dogs, ducks laughed themselves silly at private jokes that humans weren't a party to, and the ubiquitous seagulls squawked and stole chips from holidaymakers. In short, an idyllic spot that gave poor old, soon to be redeveloped, Ashwood Hall a run for its money. Up in the cloudless cobalt-blue sky, a hot-air balloon hissed back at the swans as it sailed majestically over the pitch.

Down on the ground, in the car park, the Ashwood entourage was arriving. Dennis and Mike strode over to meet their counterparts, while the lads headed for the changing rooms. A gaggle of Pebbleton players stood on and around the parched square, prodding bits of turf with serious expressions. Others greeted their opponents and showed them round the facilities, such as they were. The pavilion was small and cosy. It had two changing rooms, home and away, each with a shower, and two lavatory blocks – one nice one for the ladies, with freshly cut flowers, and one grotty one for the men, with the usual, tragic blue-gel air fresheners, fighting for their lives in a pungent lake of stale urine. A poster of a semi-naked Pamela Anderson, corrugated by years of condensation, hung in a mouldy frame above one of the urinals for reasons we can only speculate on – and hope against hope that we are wrong.

At the front of the pavilion was a small bar with Formica tables and chairs, and a television in the corner. Virtually every square inch of the walls was covered by ancient picture frames showing teams from previous eras, some in sepia, some in black and white, some in 1960s faded colour and some bang up to date, curiously devoid of the players' names. This, explained a Pebbleton player with obvious embarrassment, was because the child protection people had declared the naming of junior players as no longer acceptable, on the grounds that any passing paedophiles might show an unhealthy interest. How sad, that future generations would scrutinize a team photograph full of anonymous, forgotten players, and not be able to identify a great-granddad, uncle, or distant relative. Each photo was not only a record of the many teams that had called this lovely spot their spiritual home, but also lasting proof of how ridiculous men's hairstyles were in the 1970s. Any space not reserved for photo frames was dedicated to signed bats. There were hundreds of them. It seemed that any passing stranger would be asked to sign a bat, judging by the amount of the things. Had a pipistrelle strayed into the building through an old air vent one night, they'd have probably insisted on signing that too.

Paul Beenie's gaze turned from the walls to the bar. Behind it, two fat ladies – maybe even the ones made famous by the bingo call – were busy taking the cling film off several plates of food. They interrupted their labours to say hello. Cricket people were nice, he thought to himself. Crazy, yes, eccentric, certainly, but nice nevertheless. Out on the car park, Amanda Beenie lugged the cool box, two foldaway chairs and the parasol from the back of the car and struggled over to the spot she and her husband had chosen, up on the bank, side-on to the wicket, so they could see how fast Ben was bowling. Paul waved and directed her a little to the left. He liked to be of use.

Bang on time, Dougie Lennox-Cameron's car swung through the front gates and crunched across the gravel to a parking spot that saved him from having to walk too far to the changing rooms. Barry had phoned him as he was driving through Bristol to inform him that he would be standing in for his son, who had contracted what they suspected was Norovirus, but was perfectly okay, other than that stuff was coming out of him with alarming regularity from both ends. Dougie didn't seem overly concerned on hearing this, for two reasons. He had sent Jeremy to a private boarding school in order to toughen him up a bit, a notion that divided loyalties at the club. Some thought it a good idea, while others questioned the sense of it when the Lennox-Camerons lived next door to the school. A dose of Norovirus wasn't pleasant, but it all came within the remit of Dougie's toughening up process. The boy would survive. Besides, the second reason Dougie wasn't unduly concerned is that he now got a chance to play cricket himself – something he didn't think he'd be able to do if the regular squad was fit. It was galling to be first reserve, and to pay a fortune for a week's stay at a Devon hotel with no promise of a game. One man's meat was another man's poison, as Dougie would often say. Shame the other man was his son, but that was life. Anyway, it was his son's fault for catching the winter vomiting bug in the height of summer. The boy was obviously a fool who didn't know one season from the next. Scotsmen, as Dougie would often remind people, were born pragmatic. The only downside, of course, was that he had to wear Jeremy's kit. Dougie quite often looked a clown on a cricket pitch, so he could have done without adding to the image by dressing as one.

Half an hour later, the players from both sides were changed and ready to do battle. The two captains met in the middle and tossed a coin, and Matt chose to bat, rather than go into the field with one player still missing.

Without further ado, the fielders took their places, and Matt and Ollie strode purposefully out to the wicket, bats swinging. After five overs, things were going well, with both batsmen still at the crease, and a handful of runs in the bag. Then someone noticed an intruder on the pitch. A tall young man with long, curly hair, dressed in a T-shirt and cut-off jeans had begun walking from the boundary rope towards the square. Draped around his neck was a huge sheet of some description, and as he got closer, the curious observers in the pavilion and on the pitch realized that it was a flag. The man, who was hidden behind a pair of reflective chrome-finish sunglasses, was wearing what they could now make out as an Ashwood Cricket Club flag, the very same one that disappeared from the flagpole at Ashwood Hall earlier that season. He was currently around five feet away from the umpire, who stopped play momentarily while he ascertained who this uninvited guest was. It was hardly Lord's, but even so, he had witnessed streaking incidents before at village cricket level, and he didn't want it happening here. Ignoring polite requests to vacate the area, the Flag Man continued past the nonplussed umpire and resting batsman, and then strode down the wicket itself, his arms at first aloft and then spread out to the sides like a giant capital T, palms open and hands like those on a religious Michelangelo painting – the Messiah come to visit his people, returned from the dead.

Leo Jackman had finally arrived, and it was the Leo Jackman they were hoping wouldn't show up.

Leo was a talented cricketer and a manic livewire with an irrepressible spirit, but earlier that year, he had gone off the rails, and some feared for his sanity. The periods of lucidity were becoming less and less, and bouts of bizarre behaviour more and more commonplace. Things finally came to a head when he was overheard advocating the joys of crack cocaine to the under-thirteens squad during an outdoor practice session, and he was asked to leave the club and not darken its door again. However, a softening of attitudes prevailed, and after promises were made to clean up acts, Leo was allowed to work behind the bar and do odd jobs for cash, to augment his meagre income, on condition he never again chatted to minors about the advantages of facing aggressive bowlers whilst high as a kite on illegal substances. One such odd job was to repaint the front door of the clubhouse midnight blue, after a decade of it being a vile and repugnant lime green, so in a sense, Leo *had* been allowed to darken the club's door again, but in a good way. Things seemed to be improving, and the lad appeared to be slowly getting back to his old, loveable, unpunctual, scatterbrained self and rejoining the fold, but this strange entrance today had given everyone who witnessed it grave cause for concern.

Matt Wood, the batsman on strike at the pavilion end, called Leo over and had a discreet word, and afterwards Leo headed for the far boundary rope once more and disappeared over the hillock, promising to be back in time for if he had to bat at number eight. Thankfully, given his present state of mind, Leo was not required, and the first six batsmen saw it through the 40 overs first half, chalking up a half-decent 122 runs. Not at all bad for a team with a communal hangover that would have hospitalized lesser men.

Tea followed, and the hot topic of the bar room over mini sausage rolls, slices of quiche and chocolate éclairs was divided between the Pebbleton players eager to ask about the strange Messiah figure who briefly interrupted the game, and those who were fascinated by the chunky-looking fellow in drag. Shaun, who had been forced to wear the woman's dress on the previous day as a forfeit for misdirecting the car to Stoke-on-Trent, was still sporting it proudly. They could only surmise that he enjoyed the look.

41

The second half of the match saw Ashwood's jaded players beginning to wilt badly, after their promising start. It was one thing batting, but quite another having to run around after the ball in the sticky heat of a decent summer's day, especially as the mysterious Messiah, Leo, had not shown up, in spite of his promise to Matt to be back towards the end of the first half to bat if required. Pebbleton had a pair of powerful openers who knew their pitch intimately, and exploited this knowledge to the full, and it took far too long to winkle them out. Beeno was summoned by Matt Wood to take over the bowling, alongside Jay Taylor, for the simple tactical reason that they were the only two bowlers who didn't have hangovers, and within half an hour they had succeeded in disposing of the next two batsmen. The fifth fellow, a huge, gorilla of a man and a big hitter, tried to belt one of Jay's slow, spinning deliveries into the next county, but only succeeded in skying it so high that people enjoying the hot-air balloon excursion were now beginning to look extremely nervous. The ball eventually began its homeward journey, and down below, Dougie Lennox-Cameron, squashed into his son's whites and feeling very uncomfortable indeed, was following its trajectory like a hawk, constantly adjusting his position so that he'd be right under it when it got within the final ten feet. Unfortunately, his movements were hampered by the fact that his trousers were made for a dwarf, and not the fifteen-stone beer drinker he was, and having realized too late that he was some five feet short of his required destination, he took a flying leap, and to his utter amazement – Dougie would be the first to admit that he was not the best fielder in the world, or even in his cul-de-sac – he hung on to the rocketing, rock-hard ball and crashed into the even harder ground with it still safely in his possession. Dazed by the mighty impact of self on pitch, his shoulder throbbing horribly, he nevertheless raised the ball in triumph, just to make sure the umpire didn't suspect him of secretly dropping the thing. Immediately, the entire ground erupted in spontaneous applause, and Dougie dragged himself off the ground to acknowledge his public, grinning inanely, desperate to hide the intense pain surging through his fat freckled frame. It was only then that he realized why the applause had been so great. A meagre handful of purists, such as Dennis and Mike, were clapping because he'd taken a half-decent catch. Virtually everyone else was clapping because Dougie had burst out of his son's trousers so spectacularly that little of them remained; just a few scattered rags, in fact, floating off across the pitch in the breeze. Dougie stood there, taking a bow, ball in hand, with not a stitch on below the waist, his stubby little member poking out at a jaunty angle beneath his considerable beer belly. Jeremy's tiny trousers and box-shorts had simply exploded under the strain, and worse still, his small shirt wasn't anywhere near long enough to pull down for modesty-preservation purposes. Unless a kindly umpire obliged with a spare jumper, Dougie would have to walk all the way back to the pavilion baring all. Thankfully, for everyone's sake, help came, albeit far too slowly for the red-faced Scot.

Then, just as Ashwood looked to be in with a chance, one of the fat ladies ran onto the pitch carrying a cordless phone. Gasping for breath – for she was not built for exercise, but for éclair consumption – she handed the instrument to the nearest umpire, who listened to it for a while, and looked very grave as he did so. He called for Matt Wood, who trotted over, followed by several others, curious to see what all the drama

43

was about. Then the captain immediately ran back to the pavilion to see Dennis, Barry and Mike, who were enjoying a gin and tonic each on the balcony.

'It's Jackass,' said Matt breathlessly. 'He's been eaten by a lion.'

Chapter 5

Leo and the Lion

'If you could write down, say, five hundred ways to snuff it in Devon,' said Mike, who was sat in the Seaview Hotel bar the following day, at lunchtime, 'I doubt that being eaten by a lion would have figured among them.'

'He was damned lucky *not* to die,' said Dennis, fastening up his new lilac cable-knit pullover to shield him from the draft created when Barry wandered in, leaving the door wide open behind him. 'I told you that lad was having mental problems didn't I? It's probably been exacerbated by all the cannabis he's been sniffing.'

'I don't think they sniff it,' said Mike, who wasn't an expert himself.

Barry, in smart Ashwood tracksuit, sat down beside them.

'I've just been on the phone to the hospital,' he said. 'They won't allow us to visit as he's not out of the woods yet by a long chalk. He's lost half an arm and he's plastered in nasty deep gashes, apparently.'

'Oh bugger!' sighed Mike. 'He was our best pace bowler, when he was compos mentis.'

'Have you been able to find out what happened?' asked Dennis.

'More or less, yes. Apparently, he wandered off again, as you know, and ended up at the small zoo down the road. People there said he was singing at the top of his voice, but they thought he was just drunk and had escaped from a football match.'

'What was he singing?' asked Mike.

'The policeman said he was singing Johnny B. Goode,' said Barry.

'Thought so,' said Mike. 'He's always singing that. It's the only bloody song he knows all the way through. He always does it at the club karaoke night. I wish he'd learn another one. Then what happened?'

'The copper said he started rapping to the lion, you know, like that Emineminem chap. Then he grabbed hold of a painter and decorator's ladder, while he was having a break from doing up the cafeteria, and ran off with it. He placed it up against the netting and climbed up it, and when he got to the top, he shouted, "To infinity and beyond!", and jumped onto a grassy bank in the lion's enclosure. The decorator told the copper that it had hurt his legs, Jackass's I mean, not the decorator's, but then he stood up and seemed to be calling the lion to him, like that chap in the bible story, Andrex. Or am I thinking of Andromeda? You know, when he gets the nail out of its paw and they become friends. We did it at school.'

'You got a nail out of a lion's paw at school?' asked Dennis.

'That was Androcles, you cretin,' said Mike.

'Whatever. Anyway, it seemed to jump up at him and rest his paws on Jackass's shoulders, and just look at him for a bit, like they were mates, according to the painter and decorator, and then it suddenly ripped half of his bloody arm off.'

'Bloody hell!' said Dennis, shuddering at the thought.

'I suppose we'll have to call the tour off now,' said Mike. 'I presume his parents have been informed.'

'Matt's done it,' said Barry. 'His mother flipped. She's gone mental.'

'Her as well then,' said Dennis.

'We should go on with the tour regardless,' suggested Barry. 'What's the point in going home? It won't make Leo's arm grow back will it? Besides, it's what he would have wanted.'

He can *still* want it, you prat, he's not dead you know,' frowned Mike. 'He's just got some bits missing. And have you noticed, what's best for the deceased almost always seems to conveniently coincide with what the relatives want? Old Jim's died. Let's still go on that Caribbean cruise and not bother going to his funeral then. It's what he would have wanted. Would he bollocks!'

'Barry does have a point though, Mike,' said Dennis. 'Poor old Leo is stuck down here in intensive care. We're here too, for the rest of the week. If we went home, there'd be no one to visit him. I vote we carry on and send a lad or two to sit with him after the game, as soon as the doctors reckon he's well enough. And sorry to sound pragmatic and uncaring here, but it's cost us all a small fortune to stay here for a week, remember, and I daresay the money's not refundable if we go home early. This is our last hurrah, remember? We haven't even seen a complete game of cricket yet either, what with yesterday being called off when we heard the dreadful news. I reckon we stood a fair chance of winning that game as well, once Beeno and Jay came on.'

'Yes, I do,' said Mike. 'I think that umpire overreacted, deciding to call off the game because our bowler had been part-eaten by a lion. It's not like it started raining heavily or anything, and we were in a fairly strong position at that point. He should have asked us if we wanted to continue with ten players really. I suspect he wasn't as neutral as he made out. Anyway, it's water under the bridge now and best forgotten. How's young Jeremy, by the way?'

'He's learnt his lesson, and he's raring to go,' Barry assured him. 'And talking of which, we need to go too. Lenchford-on-Sea is seven miles away, so we need to make tracks. We have a full team today if you count Dougie. He's popped to the local sports shop and got himself and his son some new kit, so hopefully we won't have to see what he keeps under his bloody kilt today. It put me off my breakfast sausage, I don't mind telling you.'

'Chipolata more like,' added Mike, draining his second brandy.

'Quite!' agreed Dennis. 'There were too many blasted willies on show yesterday, from what I've been hearing. At least they all got a good night's sleep last night, so they should look a bit sharper in the field today than they were at Pebbleton. I *was* pleased with their behaviour after the game for once though. I know we used to have a bit of fun on tour, but that lot were like bloody animals that first night, and by that I don't mean fluffy little hamsters. I was thinking more of wild bulls in small china shops. The stories I heard yesterday. Bloody hell! But credit where it's due. Matto had a word, and they ended up going for a curry and an early night. Mrs Grainger doesn't want to be cleaning up piles of sick when she's just buried her mother does she?'

The Elder Statesmen rose unsteadily to their feet and trooped outside where they were met by the team, resplendent in their new tour T-shirts and smart blue tracksuits. All but Jeremy, that was. He was wearing a rather fetching floral mini dress, and Matto's girlfriend, Karen, had expertly picked out the turquoise in the dress and matched it with a subtle dash of eye shadow. To complete the transformation, she'd been to work with her heated rollers and now Jeremy had a lovely, wavy bob. Just to compound the poor lad's misery, he was then ordered to pop into the corner shop a few yards from the hotel entrance to buy newspapers and chewing gum for the team. When he protested that enough was enough, Matt reminded him that failure to carry out this forfeit would result in him being dropped in favour of Barry the coach, who could still, just about, wield a bat and chuck a ball. With heavy heart, Jeremy sloped off with cash in hand to get the ordeal over with. He entered the cramped little shop, selected his items and stood at the counter, waiting to pay. The proprietor was busy on the phone, which seemed to prolong the mental torture in the cruellest way. Eventually, the man turned to face him, and a twinkle of recognition flashed in the shop assistant's eyes.

'Jemima,' he said, blushing slightly. 'How arc you?' He took Jeremy's ten-pound note and scanned the confectionery and newspapers, all the while staring, love-struck into Jeremy's turquoise-tinted, sad brown eyes. Jeremy now wanted to die, and quickly.

'Look,' continued the Pierre's Pier Bar bouncer after a lengthy pause. 'I hope you don't mind me saying this, but why would a beautiful woman like you want to become a man? You're gorgeous as you are.'

He handed back Jeremy's change, his tattooed, ham-like hand lingering on top of Jeremy's briefly as he did so.

Dennis, Mike and Barry set up camp on the boundary rope. Once they had fathomed out how to assemble their new foldaway chairs, and then bandaged Mike's finger, they slumped into them and Dennis poured Mike and Barry a tea each from his new flask, which boasted a smart, cable-knit sleeve designed to keep the tea even hotter. Barry handed out the newspapers – *The Times* for Mike, *Telegraph* for Dennis, and *Daily Mirror* for himself. The corner shop didn't have *The Sport*, Jeremy said.

'Did you remember your suntan lotion?' asked Dennis. 'We don't want bloody skin cancer. My skin is shot after sixty years of watching cricket.'

'I've got some here you can use,' said Mike, handing him an orange tube.

'And sorry to be cheeky,' said Dennis, 'but I don't suppose you have any of that lotion for the midges, do you?'

'For Christ's sake, let the midges find their own lotion,' chipped in Barry, a little distracted and preoccupied with trying to locate the sports pages. Mike and Dennis eyed each other with a look that asked, 'Did he actually mean that or was it a joke?' With Barry, one was never entirely sure. They decided to let it pass.

'I had a bloody call from my mother back at the hotel,' said Barry, five minutes later, apropos of nothing. 'She was asking about Jackass and I told her he was okay but he'd had half his arm ripped off, and they couldn't sew it back on because the lion had eaten it. She said my brother's car has had to go into the garage to have something fitted to it. She said the egg basket had gone. Lord knows what she's on about.'

'What?' queried Mike. 'What do you mean, egg basket?'

'I'm not entirely sure what she was on about, as I say,' admitted Barry. 'She's nearly ninety you know. He's got a

Renault something or other. French thing. Maybe they fit them with egg baskets, because it tends to be rural doesn't it? France?'

Mike gave Dennis another look.

'She said he'd got her some stuff for the lavatory. Ortisan I think she said it was. Only it was past its sell-by date.'

'What *are* you blathering on about?' asked Mike, who was trying to digest an article on liver transplants and had read the same sentence eight times already.

'Ortisan. Out of date,' explained Barry. 'She said she put it in the lavvy and there was no smell at all coming off it, so she's going to take it back to the chemists on Saturday.'

'Bloody hell!' said Dennis under his breath.

'She did tell me one funny thing though,' continued Barry, gamely, seemingly oblivious to his friends' disinterest. 'My brother, Tony, the one with the Renault, cleaned his teeth yesterday and he complained to his wife – Jacquie her name is – that his toothpaste was off, and she said, what do you mean off, and when they looked at the tube, they realized it was Vagisil.'

'What the hell is Vagisil?' asked Dennis, giving up on his newspaper until Barry's famed pointless anecdotes had run their course.

'Not sure,' Barry admitted, 'but I think it's for women, down below, judging by the name.'

'Bloody hell!' said Mike, shuddering at the prospect. 'I wonder if she accidentally cleaned her doo-dah with toothpaste as well. I'm told that makes their eyes water, women. My mate Glenn, who's got too much testosterone in my opinion, used to put a little tiny bit of Ultrabrite on his finger, prior to stimulating his wife's whatsit, and he reckoned it sent her wild.'

'Well I never,' said Dennis, fascinated. 'I wonder how he discovered that trick?'

'Lord knows,' said Mike, 'but he came unstuck. He had a dirty weekend with his secretary, apparently, in Brighton, and he thought he'd try the old toothpaste ploy on her, so he did, and seconds later she was on fire down below, like someone had put acid on it or something, and when she realized what he'd done, she whacked the radio alarm across his head and blacked his eye. Then she got up and caught the next train back to Brum.'

'Christ!' said Barry. 'It must not have suited her. She should have tried that Sensodyne stuff instead.'

'Can I read my newspaper now, do you think?' asked Mike. 'If you wouldn't mind.'

'Feel free,' said Barry, hurt. After all, it was Mike who'd brought up the Ultrabrite incident, not him.

Mike resumed his reading, but was further interrupted by the arrival of the teams on the pitch. Ashwood had lost the toss and been made to field. Out on the boundary line, a creature of indeterminate sex stood shivering in a floral frock.

'Head gasket!' said Dennis suddenly, as if he'd experienced a Eureka moment.

'What?' asked Mike, still grappling with the same sentence he'd read over and over again.

'Head gasket,' repeated Dennis, smiling now. 'And Ortisan is for constipation. I had to take some once on a Nile cruise. That's how I remember.'

Big Jim and Beeno opened the bowling, and made an immediate breakthrough, skittling out the opener for a duck. The Lenchford player stormed back into the pavilion, examining his bat intensely as he stormed. Lenchford's number three passed him en route to the crease and offered his condolences, and was curtly told to fuck off. There was obviously something wrong with the bat and the opener was mightily displeased. In fact, it was not only his bat that displeased him. Judging by the commotion emanating from the home changing room just after he entered it, he didn't much care for that either. It sounded as if he were attempting to demolish it singlehandedly with his malfunctioning bat.

Dennis, Mike and Barry smiled wryly. They'd seen it all before. Batsmen are never out. All LBW decisions are erroneous; all run outs are the result of the myopic imbeciles wearing the white cow gowns, and when the stumps fly out of the ground…well, then it was the bat's fault. The Elder Statesmen ignored the cussing and blinding behind them and concentrated on the view, which was nothing short of picture-postcard idyllic.

The pitch itself was a work of art. The Lenchford groundsman was a true artist, it had to be said; he was the Pissarro of the Pitch, the Warhol of the Wicket, or the Gauguin of the Grass, depending on one's preference. His striped outfield gave Lord's a run for its money, and by all accounts the wicket was to die for. White picket fencing skirted the old white pavilion, and there were hanging baskets and pots of flowers everywhere. Butterflies fluttered, bees buzzed, swifts and swallows skimmed the grass, and the regular thwack of leather on willow (and the occasional shinbone) added the icing to an already wonderful cake. The sky was cobalt and virtually cloudless, as it had been on the previous day, but now it was a degree or two warmer. The hot-air balloon was noticeable only by its absence, but in its place was a small Cessna twin-engined aircraft, dragging behind it a large banner expounding the delights of Sunburne-on-Sea, or some such resort, farther down the coast.

Out on the perfect pitch, Big Jim had taken another wicket, but judging by the commotion, at a cost. The number three batsman had skied one of Jim's lightning deliveries, and it looked for a moment as if it would clear the boundary rope. Jeremy stood, as his father had done on the previous day, nervously watching the trajectory of the ball, and realized to his horror that it was heading his way, something no fielder relishes, if the truth were known. Dennis, Barry and Mike watched, knuckles in mouths (their own, of course), as the little public schoolboy shimmied this way and that, his pretty dress artily backlit, and showing off his chubby little legs through the gossamer-thin silky fabric – a little like the iconic photograph of the young Lady Diana

55

Spencer, but somehow not nearly as appealing. The ball, travelling at something like 80 miles per hour, thwacked into Jeremy's hands, and much to the lad's delight, and against all the odds, he held on to it. However, joy quickly turned to agony, and Jeremy sank to the ground, wailing like a scalded cat. Players dashed over to see what the fuss was all about, and the Elder Statesmen, even from their distant vantage point, could see that all was not well. Matt Wood was signalling wildly to the pavilion for assistance, and his calls were answered by the St John's Ambulance man, who ran across the pitch with his bag of Band-Aids. Minutes later, a clearly distressed Jeremy was helped back to the clubhouse with his finger held aloft, his face as bloodless as his finger was bloodied. There was blood everywhere, in fact, apart from inside of him. The impact of the rock-hard ball had pretty much caused his soft little index finger to explode, and it was a sight not for the squeamish.

Those cynics who observe cricket from afar and deem it to be a boring, overly genteel sort of game, are grossly misled. This strangest of sports, this game that divides the country in a way that only Marmite can equal, may *appear* harmless from a discreet distance, but close up, a player can sometimes feel as if he has strayed onto the streets of Northern Ireland in the bad old days and found himself in the middle of a rubber-bullet battle. Anyone doubting that this is a dangerous game should stand immediately behind the nets at a training session, and watch a fast bowler launch an 80-miles-per-hour cobble at a batsman's head; a batsman who will have a split second to decide whether to hit it or duck. Those who possess slower minds are usually on a life-support machine just after that. Most wicket keepers, if you know any, will be able to show you a bruise somewhere on their body, maybe even a couple, that measure a foot in diameter, caused by missing a catch. It is a safe bet to assume that none of them will ever be concert pianists, as most of their fingers are broken and grossly misshapen. In short, cricket is not nearly as nice as it looks.

If anyone could testify to this, it was Jeremy. The St John's man had done his best, but what Jeremy needed was eight stitches, and to this end, he was shovelled into a passing ambulance and taken away with Matt's girlfriend and ex-nurse, Karen, on hand to provide moral support. Dougie, his concerned father, weighed up his parental responsibilities – in this case, the Bedside Vigil – against his chance of batting higher up the order, and chose the latter. Meanwhile, at a nearby Devonshire hospital, poor Jeremy had quite a lot of explaining to do with regard to his choice of apparel, not to mention the fact that he seemed to enjoy playing cricket in it. All in all, so far this hadn't been a tour he would remember with fondness.

Once the drama was over, a ten-man Ashwood team battled bravely on against a strong opposition. Dennis, as has been documented, was well stricken in years and would never see seventy again, and though his life was dedicated to cricket, it cannot be denied that he enjoyed the odd nap during a game. Most people at that age did, after all, and Dennis was no exception. The cricket pitch seemed to have a calming influence on him, as it does on many older people, a characteristic that cricket's critics (say that when you've had a couple) use in evidence against it. One minute, Mike would be chatting away merrily to his old friend, and the next, he found himself conversing with someone who was fast asleep.

Mike, on this particular occasion, was commenting on the Cessna appearing again, and wanted Dennis and Barry's opinion. Mike was no aviation expert – he admitted that (it might not have even been a Cessna) – but he was concerned that the aircraft's engine didn't sound tuned properly. He poked Dennis, who woke up a little confused, and asked the question.

'Sounds a bit spluttery to me,' said Barry. 'Perhaps it needs a service.'

'They do sound like that sometimes,' Dennis assured them, yawning so widely that Barry thought his old head might snap in two. 'Sounds okay to me.'

'What's that black smoke coming from the engines then?' queried Mike. 'That's not normal is it?'

'Oh bugger!' said Barry. 'The bloody engines have stopped altogether now. Can they glide, these planes?'

'I don't know,' said Dennis, 'but he's descending a bit too sharpish for my liking. Shit! He's trying to land!'

Dennis shot out of his folding chair very quickly for an elderly man who, until seconds ago, had been fast asleep. He gathered his belongings together and moved everything about two yards to the left, as if that would do him any good. Mike stood up and yelled to the players, pointing skywards as he did so. By now, the Cessna was so close that it was possible to make out the figure of the presumably incontinent pilot crossing himself and praying.

Down below, players dashed in all directions, still unsure which one was best. The Cessna's wings wobbled from side to side, everything eerily silent, now that the engines had died. It seemed to be heading for the wicket, probably because it looked like a landing strip. Seconds later, it ploughed into the ground, skidding this way and that, tearing up huge chunks of the beautifully prepared strip. Back in the pavilion, a groundsman wept. A wing tip scraped the grass, leaving a long, ploughed-up arc of brown soil. The plane spun round 180 degrees, and finally stopped, its nose rammed through the stumps at the pavilion end, and black, choking smoke beginning to belch out of the twin engines. A door opened and two men leapt out, running for their lives. Then there was a loud 'kaboom', and lots of orange flame.

The wicket was totally destroyed. An incinerated Cessna light aircraft lay on the strip with its back broken and half a wing snapped off. It was a surreal scene, like something from a Bond movie. There was only one thing to do. Once the busier-than-usual St John's Ambulance man had checked the flyers over and tended to their thankfully minor injuries, the teams decided to take tea early and call it a day. They invited the two shaken airmen to join them, as, thanks to Jeremy's accident and Nurse Karen's act of selflessness, there were two teas spare. Mike surveyed the carnage in dismay and wondered if they'd ever be able to fit a game in, before they returned to the Midlands.

'When we die, we go from earth up to heaven, if we believe our bibles,' he said, seemingly apropos of nothing. 'But when aeroplane engines die, they go from heaven down to earth. Interesting that!'

Dennis looked askance at his old friend. Sometimes, Mike could come out with the strangest observations, completely out of the blue.

'And they say cricket isn't exciting!' he sighed, pouring himself a nice cup of tea from his cable-knit flask.

Chapter 6

It Never Rains…

The breakfast room was full to overflowing on Thursday, and everyone was excited about the day's game, which was against a very small village side by the name of Bingham Magna near Lynmouth. This was quite a jaunt, compared to the previous two games, so the players were up nice and early.

Dennis, Mike and Barry were sat in the bay window, flicking through magazines that had been donated by previous guests, reading the daily newspapers and helping themselves to cereal and orange juice.

'Cornflakes anyone?' asked Dennis, who was being mother.

'No thanks,' said Barry. 'Cornflakes don't agree with me.'

'Don't agree with you about what? Religion? Politics?' asked Mike, who saw himself as a bit of a dry comedian. The comment flew harmlessly several feet above Barry's head and out of the open window, into the street.

'No need to take a paracetamol today,' Barry continued, flicking through the *Daily Mail*. The little corner shop had sold out of *Daily Mirrors* again, much to his annoyance. 'The weather's taken a turn for the worst. It's forecast heavy rain down where we're headed. Looks okay here though, at the moment. Very patchy, the rain in Devon, I always find.'

'What's that got to do with taking a paracetamol?' asked Dennis, perplexed.

'Sorry, I meant a parasol,' said Barry, who was renowned for mangling his words, and had once, to Mike's delight, complained that a sharp garden spade had nearly decapitated his foot. 'We might need an umbrella though, if this here weather forecast is accurate.'

Mike was disdainfully perusing a magazine called *Chat Break*, which had a migraine-inducing, overly busy cover featuring lots of Day-Glo pink and yellow headlines and a photo of an orange-skinned, raven-haired glamour model, who was pouting at him with lips that resembled a small dinghy. He read out some of the articles to his two friends, whether they wanted him to or not.

'Listen to this. "Malaysian man eats his own leg." I don't know where they get these stories from, I really don't. I'm sure they just make them up. What about this one? "The woman who was frightened of her ears." There's a Latin name for it, according to this. It's a rare medical condition, like when people are frightened of clowns. And how about this? "I was slim when I met my boyfriend, Darren, but he imprisoned me in his grubby flat and force-fed me for three years, and now I'm forty stone and can't get off the bed." Or there's the story about how they use whale shit to make expensive perfumes. Well, really, it beggars belief!'

'I've heard of this before,' said Dennis, confusingly referring to the previous obesity article and not the whale excrement one. 'They're called feeders. I always suspected Kevin Potts was one, but it turns out Gail just loved doughnuts and iced buns. She brought two boxes of éclairs to the cricket one time and said they were a treat for the team. The lads all politely refused them so she sat in her fold-up chair and scoffed all sixteen of them that afternoon, at a rate of one every three minutes, give or take. I wouldn't mind, but she did this quite often, I learnt later, and she knew damned well the lads didn't like éclairs. Anyway, then she popped to the bar for a Diet Coke, came back, sat in the chair, and it collapsed. Talk about embarrassing. It was only from Aldi, but even so, it should have held her weight really. I told her to take it back as it wasn't fit for the purpose, but she said she didn't want to for some reason.'

'Why is every headline in the *Mail* about three things?' asked Barry, again apropos of nothing, which was Barry's default setting. 'Have you ever noticed? Look, here's one. "David Mellor, *that* weekend, and a close encounter with a zebra." Hang on, here's another one on page fourteen. "Simon Cowell, a rather grubby sports bra, his domineering mother and *that* spat with Gerry Haliwell." Oh, that's four things. Anyway, you get the idea, and the other thing they do is ask weird questions all the time to get you to read the article.'

'Such as?' asked Dennis.

'Here's a typical one,' said Barry, turning to the lifestyle section near the back. '"Could celery hold the cure to testicular cancer?" And when you read on, it'll almost certainly say, no, it couldn't. See what I mean? It's just to suck you in.'

'I do,' said Dennis. 'One year red wine is good for you, the next year it'll kill you. I wish the scientists would make their minds up. Best thing is just do what you flipping well like and to hell with them. I was just reading the sports pages of *The Telegraph* when you interrupted me. It said that the Spanish have a new nickname for Wayne Rooney. It's – hang on a bit, let me find it again…oh yes, "The Freckled Demon with a Stomach Full of Gunpowder." Well, it's not very catchy is it?'

Mercifully, Dennis's mobile phone rang at that point. He sat listening to the caller for a while, and nodded in agreement every now and then, his sad old face looking ever more despondent. He thanked the caller and placed the phone back into its purple cable-knit protective case.

'Game's off, gentlemen!' he announced to the whole breakfast room. A chorus of sighs and theatrical moans greeted him.

'Apparently, it's absolutely bucketed it down over there and the wicket is covered in puddles. There's no way it's playable, according to the groundsman. It's only a small village club, he said, and they don't own any covers. Looks like you lot have a day to yourselves, and hopefully tomorrow's game with Barnbridge will still be on.'

Thankfully, the weather in Pitbank-on-Sea was still fairly good – just a little overcast but with no rain forecast, so after breakfast the touring party split into little groups and did whatever took their fancy.

Dennis, Mike and Barry decided to visit the local Sea Life Centre, and afterwards go for fish and chips somewhere along the front. Jay Taylor and Beeno wanted to head for the beach, play a little beach cricket, explore the rock pools and eat ice creams, to remind them of their youth, while most of the older lads quite fancied a train ride to Torquay. Dougie and Jeremy were going to have a quiet father-and-son bonding day, as Dougie didn't often get to see much of his boy, thanks to him being away at boarding school, even if it was next door. They opted for the cinema followed by lunch in a local pub. Thankfully, Jeremy was spared the floral dress, being as it was a day of rest, even though the players had unanimously voted for him yet again for getting his finger cut to ribbons, which in turn meant that his cricket was well and truly over for the week, and they were down to ten men again. Unless someone did something even more dick-headed in the interim, they warned, he may have to resume his drag act on the following day and also fill in the scorebook – something most players hated with a passion. Jeremy need not have worried. That floral dress was going to be spoilt for choice, come Friday breakfast time.

After breakfast, Jay and Beeno made their way to the beach on foot, armed with a couple of bats. They stopped off at a toy-shop en route to buy a bag of cheap tennis balls and a child's set of cricket stumps, and then spent an hour or so belting the balls all over the beach, much to the annoyance of the sunbathers, who must have thought they'd accidentally chosen a wartime Normandy beach by accident. One well-struck ball hit an elderly woman in the back of the head and forced her face into her cornet. Another made a passing Yorkshire terrier yelp. At this point, Jay suggested that Beeno only played defensive strokes, but after a token few, he resorted to battering every ball Jay bowled at him into the sea, just to demonstrate his dominance over the bowling attack. Then, when it was his turn to bowl, he'd do so with such ferocity that the balls would end up hundreds of yards away if Jay missed them with the bat. It was Jay's idea to end the session after one of Beeno's rockets felled a toddler making a sandcastle with his bodybuilder father, and things got heated. Suddenly deciding that somewhere else was probably where they ought to be, the boys decamped with a fair amount of haste and legged it in the direction of the rock pools, over to the right of the beach, next to the cliffs. They paddled around in the warm, shallow pools for a good hour, upending countless stones in their search for crabs and having a lovely, innocent, old-fashioned time. Then they wandered over to the area next to the pools that was covered in foul-smelling, fly-infested, slimy seaweed, and began throwing strands of it at each other. Jay found a tenpin-bowling-ball-sized, slimy grey and yellow rock-like object amongst the weeds and old strands of blue rope, and threw it at Beeno, who bowled it back at him with expert accuracy, nearly taking his head off. Strangely, the slimy ball wasn't nearly as heavy as it appeared, so the next ten minutes were spent playing a game of catch, until both lads were plastered in foul-smelling slime, sand and mud, like proper children used to be before computer games were invented. Exhausted, they called a truce and sat down on the beach to have a rest.

'I've just had a brilliant idea,' announced Jay. 'I'm going to take this ball of sea snot back to the hotel and put it in Gareth's luggage, to get him back for the Pink Bat Grip Incident, or PBGI for short.'

'Good idea,' agreed Beeno. 'I'll take some of the slimy seaweed to go with it then.'

The boys gathered together their belongings and headed back to the hotel, the ball of sea snot and the slimy weeds discreetly hidden in the toy-shop carrier bag, so as not to arouse suspicion.

'How come your mom and dad didn't want to come this week?' asked Beeno, as he emptied Gareth's kitbag all over the floor of his and Jay's room.

'Oh, they did want to,' replied Jay, 'but dad's got some problems so they couldn't.'

'What sort of problems?' asked Beeno, as he created a nice, even layer of stinking, slimy seaweed on the bottom of the empty kitbag.

'Well, I'm not really supposed to talk about it, dad said,' said Jay, sighing. He picked up the huge ball of sea snot and placed it carefully inside the bag, and, ever the perfectionist, removed it again, and instead placed it inside Gareth's helmet, an action which appeared to lift his spirits considerably, as both boys agreed that the snot ball was a perfect fit.

'Why can't you talk about it?' probed Beeno, who was not known for his tact. 'Are they gettin' divorced or summat?'

'No, no, nothing like that,' Jay assured him. 'No, it's my dad's business. He's been struggling with it for a couple of years now. He does graphic design and stuff for local companies, and 'cause of the recession – whatever that is – he hasn't had much work from his customers. He reckons they all try to do their own adverts and brochures and stuff to save money, and he reckons they're shit. He's always moaning about the spelling errors and bad punctuation and stuff. It drives him mad. I think he's losing the plot, I really do.'

'Why, what's he do?'

'Well, he rants at the telly for a start, and he keeps showin' me bad home-done adverts in the free papers that are full of mistakes. He says no one would do their own brain surgery to save a few quid, but for some reason, folks think they can take their own photos, just 'cause they own a Nikon, and write their own text, 'cause everybody knows how to write, and put together their own ads just 'cause they've got a PC, but they can't.'

'Why can't they?'

''Cause they can't bloody spell for a start. He showed me one the other day for a tattoo parlour in Stourbridge. The place was called 'The Skin Your In' which is a shit name anyway, but he was pissing himself laughing because they'd spelt the word *you're*, as in 'you are' wrong, and instead spelt it like *your*, as in 'your turn'.

Beeno stared at his friend quizzically. He had no idea what he was on about, as spelling was not a strong point of his either.

68

'So?'

'Well, you wouldn't want a tattoo done by a bloke who couldn't even spell his shop name properly would you? How would you feel if you'd saved up fifty quid to have 'I Love Alexandra' written on your arm and when you got home, you discovered that it actually said 'I Love Alexander'? You'd have to go through your whole life with a long-sleeved shirt on in case folks thought you were a gayboy.'

'God! I see what you mean,' said Beeno, shuddering at the thought. 'If I'd have realized how important spelling was, I might have listened more in English. I never thought of that!'

He threw the remaining strands of seaweed into the bag, and then began to arrange Gareth's clothing neatly on top of it.

'So why didn't your mom and dad come then?' he asked again.

'Which bit of, "I'm not supposed to talk about it" didn't you understand?' asked Jay, with a mock severity. 'Look Beeno, keep this to yourself, 'cause he doesn't want folks knowing his business, but he's hardly earned a penny in weeks so he can't really afford to go on cricket tours, can he? He wanted me to go so I didn't miss out, but he couldn't really afford it, I know that, so I've been feeling guilty as hell. I went to bed the other night and I heard them talking downstairs. They're thinking of selling our house and getting a smaller one because he's thirty grand in debt with not much money coming in.'

'Oh shit!'

'Exactly. I think I'm going to give him the money I saved from my job at the café to help pay for this week.'

'That was for your new bat, wasn't it?'

'Ah well!' said Jay stoically. 'Anyway, let's talk about cheerful things instead. Gareth is really gonna be pissed off when he opens this bag. It bloody reeks! His clean cricket whites will stink like Grimsby docks in a heatwave.'

They zipped the bag up and returned it to where they had found it, just outside Gareth's room, both of them giggling uncontrollably at the thought of his face when he discovered the foul sea-snot ball sitting snugly, a perfect fit in his helmet. They then imagined him having to wear the helmet on a boiling summer's day, while he batted for hours at the crease, and their laughter became so intense that their sides ached, and they had to kneel on the floor, clutching their stomachs. When their laughing fit subsided, they also started to experience that strange frisson of excitement – as happens with any good prank – brought on by the very real threat of retaliation by Gareth, in response to their own act of retaliation for the PBG incident. That, pondered Jay later, as the lads enjoyed a lemonade at Rick's Milk Bar, was the trouble with wars. They tended to escalate, with each side upping the ante and refusing to give up, often at a terrible cost to both parties. They clinked their glasses together and vowed to keep a watchful eye on the Welshman for the rest of the week.

Chapter 7

Quiet. Almost Too Quiet.

Jay and Beeno observed Gareth's demeanour as he strode into the breakfast room on Friday morning, the day after the snot ball was planted. As they did so, they giggled and kicked each other under the table, the way children in their first year at secondary school do during sex education lessons. Gareth wished them a good morning, but not, as far as the lads could tell, with any hint of irony or sarcasm in his voice. This meant one of two things. Either he hadn't delved into his kitbag yet, which was probably the case, or he was a consummate actor.

Dennis, Mike and Barry were next to arrive, and Dennis seized the opportunity to address the team, before they all dispersed to collect their belongings.

'Gentlemen, listen up! A couple of points. Barnbridge today. The weather forecast is excellent, which is good news. I hope we are all rested and ready for battle. It'll be lovely to get a full day's cricket in, after three abortive attempts. Incidentally,

Matto and his good lady visited Jackass yesterday as arranged, and found him in good spirits, considering a lion had removed half of his arm. The only slightly concerning thing was that he kept telling Matto that he hoped his arm would grow back quickly as he was needed on the HMS *Victory* that afternoon. Karen puts it down to the drugs he's on, but she didn't make it clear whether she meant the legal ones supplied by the hospital or his own recreational stuff. Anyway, his folks arrived yesterday and they'll be visiting regularly, so he won't be on his own.'

'He's never on his own anyway,' said Shaun, who was finally dressed in something befitting his gender. 'He's always got the other Leo Jackass to talk to.'

'Yes, thank you, Shaun.'

'He's *armless* enough!' piped up Jeremy, raising his arm as if trying to answer a question in class, his battered index finger doing a passable impression of a very small mummified glove puppet.

'Yes, very poor taste indeed, thank you, Jeremy. I just hope that you are never eaten by a lion. Incidentally, I note that you too are in male apparel today. So who's inherited the dress?'

'That'll be me,' said Jeremy's dad, Dougie, strolling into the breakfast room in the floral dress, bang on cue. Those who thought that the vision of Shaun wearing that same dress was the most hideous thing they had ever witnessed were forced to think again. Dougie, with his fat, white, tattooed, freckly body and four-day-old ginger stubble, had taken things to a whole new level of grossness that would have caused weakerstomached people to reacquaint themselves with their full English. A round of wolf-whistles and spontaneous applause greeted the shameless Scot, who gave them a twirl. Even Dennis, often po-faced throughout such tomfoolery, had a smirk on his face.

'And why, dare we enquire,' he continued, 'are *you* in drag today?'

Jeremy, who seemed to be conquering his fear of public speaking, explained on his father's behalf.

'Well, we had the day off as you know, so me and dad went to the pictures and for something to eat, and it was still quite early so he decided that we should go on the bus to the market in Middleton Saint Katherine, which is three miles down the road. Dad said he knew this area like the back of his hand because he used to work here before he met my mother. We came out of the pub and he'd had more than a couple as usual (cue cheers from the rowdier element sat at the table in the bay window), and he told me about the number 26 bus that takes you there, so he asked this bloke how much it was to catch the bus to the midweek market, and he said it was a quid each.'

'I'm losing the will to live here. Get on with it,' shouted Shaun, of the bay-window gang.

'Sorry! So dad wanted to wait in the bus shelter across the road because there was a little rain shower and he was only wearing a T-shirt, and then the number 26 came and we jumped on and paid the man two quid and—'

'Flippin' heck, Jeremy, brevity is the soul of wit,' shouted Mike.

'Sorry! So the bus drove off and dad fell asleep and started snoring, so—'

'For fuck's sake!' added Shaun.

'Sorry, so I'm thinking, dad said this place was three miles away, and I've been sat on this bus now for an hour and dad's fast asleep and snoring really loud, and there's no sign of Middleton Saint Katherine, so I woke him up, and he was a bit groggy, and—'

'I'm going to punch your head in, in a minute,' Shaun assured him.

'Sorry! So he looks out of the window and says, "This number 26 is going all round the bloody Wrekin to get there, and it never used to. It always used to be just four stops and then you were there, and this bloody thing seems to be doing a detour through most of Devon." Anyway, it was starting to get dark, and finally, two and a half hours later, we ended up in Middleton Saint Katherine and the market was finished and it was really, really dark now, so dad didn't know this place like the back of his hand after all, and that's why he's wearing the dress.'

'You are the world's most boring and useless storyteller,' screamed Shaun. 'You haven't explained that properly at all. You missed out the punchline, you bloody turd.'

'Oh yeah, sorry, sorry,' continued Jeremy, his peachy cheeks colouring slightly. 'So we eventually got back to Pitbank-on-Sea at nine and met Shaun, Big Jim, Trento and Ollie in the pub, and dad was complaining to this local farmer chap at the bar about how they'd changed the bus route since he was last here, and the chap looked a bit puzzled by this and asked my dad where he used to catch the number 26 from, and dad said by Bagnall's Butcher's in the High Street, but because we were caught in a small shower he crossed over the road and waited for it in the number 26 bus shelter instead.'

The breakfast room clientele who had not been at the pub greeted the end of Jeremy's lengthy anecdote with stony silence. Then, gradually, the point of the story began to dawn on them, one person at a time, until the breakfast room was filled with raucous laughter. Jeremy now looked relieved, as if a weight had suddenly been lifted from his shoulders, and he acknowledged his audience with a small bow, no doubt making a mental note to work on his delivery and comedy timing in the privacy of his hotel room.

The finely honed athletes finished off their greasy breakfasts and began to reconvene out in the sunny street, where they waited for the tour vehicles to arrive. Jay, looking and sounding uncannily like Hamlet during the well-known play within a play sequence, nudged Beeno to ask if he'd been able to read anything from the Welshman's demeanour. Beeno, taking on the role of Hamlet's best mate, Horatio, confessed that he hadn't, but the time to worry was perhaps later that afternoon, once the Welshman had opened his kitbag at Barnbridge. Their shared room would need to be locked this time, that was for sure, if Batgrip Man was on the prowl and hell-bent on revenge.

Outside in the sunshine, only one detail was marring the team's happiness, and that was the injury situation. There had only been eleven men at the start of the tour, and since then, they had been dropping like flies. First to go was Kevin Potts, forced to return home due to being found *in flagrante* with a woman of the night (or in Sharon's case, the morning, noon and night). Then there was the dreadful, surreal Jackass incident, closely followed by Jeremy and his exploding index finger. Thankfully, Dougie had stepped up to the crease to help out, but he was hardly W.G. Grace – he was more like W.C. Fields if anything. Now Barry the coach would have to play, and sadly, he could well have been the original inspiration for the well-known expression, 'Those who can, do, and those who can't, teach'. It was only a matter of time before a troubled Dennis was begging the club dog to make a comeback.

Being a firm believer in the adage 'a trouble shared is a trouble halved', Dennis explained the team's predicament to the hotel's proprietor, Simon Grainger, as he sat in the lounge nursing a cup of tea, whilst waiting for Barry to bring the car round to the front of the building.

'I don't suppose you fancy a game, do you?' he asked, fully expecting a negative response.

'Well,' said Mr Grainger, rubbing his chin, 'we *are* a cricket family you know. I used to play a bit at school, but—'

'Can you get the day off?'

'It *is* my day off, actually. Jacquie is on her own today because I usually do a bit of sketching or painting on a Thursday, me being a bit of an amateur artist, and she has her day off on Fridays to see her friend Shirley for a coffee, but—'

'Can you play cricket instead of wasting your time drawing? We'll supply the kit.'

'Well, if you're desperate, and you'd have to be, but—'

'Good!' smiled Dennis. 'Go and square it with Jacquie and we'll meet you out the front in five minutes.'

And with that, he was gone before his victim could change his mind.

Barnbridge C.C. was another pretty ground with a sea view. The clubhouse was little more than a wooden hut with Spartan facilities, but Ashwood's cricketers were relaxed about such things as long as the hut contained copious quantities of tea, beer, mini sausage rolls and pork pies, triangular cheese and ham sandwiches, crisps and cake. A lavatory that actually flushed or a shower that had hot water was to them, a rare bonus and never to be taken for granted.

Inside the bustling 'away' changing room, the team members welcomed their unexpected guest player, Simon Grainger, a tall, fit, forty-something who looked as if he could handle a bat. However, two of the team's younger players were far too preoccupied with observing their devious Welsh

77

colleague's movements in the corner of the cramped little room to acknowledge Simon. They watched Gareth like a cat watches a pigeon from the bedroom window, motionless and scarcely breathing, as the object of their intense scrutiny laid down his heavy bag and proceeded to unzip it. He then removed his whites and helmet, but the ball of sea snot and the ribbons of pungent seaweed were noticeable only by their absence. Gareth had obviously removed the offending items, and surely must now be plotting his revenge, if, of course – and this was their only hope – he knew exactly who to wreak revenge upon. For all the lads knew, Gareth may have offended several other Ashwood players during the week, or, with a bit of luck, he might even have hidden the sea snot in Big Jim's kitbag as retaliation for Jim putting a dead seagull in Gareth's bag a few years back, when the two of them went on a cricket tour to Blackpool together.

Unaware that the two were watching his every move, Gareth removed his clothing and donned his whites, before strolling past Jay and Beeno on his way to the lavatory. The rancid flotsam and jetsam of the sea were certainly now residing elsewhere, but their combined scent, sadly, was not. As Gareth sailed past, he left a pungent block of stale air in his wake, prompting Adam Trent, Trento to his friends, to ask if anyone had farted, and if so, could they lay off the tuna in future.

Dennis popped his head round the door, trying his level best to avoid eye contact with the six or so players who insisted on parading around the changing room without a stitch on. He still suffered flashbacks from his own playing days, usually of being seated on a low bench minding his own business, when a naked Barry would appear and circulate amongst those present, asking for their match fees. Invariably, Barry's privates would be dangling inches from Dennis's face while his disembodied voice, somewhere above Dennis's head, would be heard demanding the sum of five pounds, like some nightmarish Bavarian butcher trying to tempt a reluctant customer with a well-past-its-sell-by Bratwurst.

'Ahem, gentlemen, as you can see, we have our friend Simon joining us today, so make him welcome,' said Dennis.

Simon was looking a tad nervous. 'Thanks folks,' he said, waving to his fellow players, who in turn ruffled his hair and patted his back. 'I have to tell you, I haven't played cricket since I was eighteen, and—'

'You'll be fine,' Dennis assured him. 'The lads will look after you!' And with that, he was gone like a thief in the night.

Back in what passed for the clubhouse, but was more like a small single-car garage, Mike and Barry were perusing the miniscule bar area in search of alcohol, the sun having gone over the yardarm hours ago as far as they were concerned. Mike opted for a brandy and dry ginger, while Barry chose a small glass of red wine that would have been better employed degreasing car body panels prior to paint-spraying. The barman handed him his change, and in a rare moment of generosity, Mike dropped it into the RNLI charity box, a small plastic affair in the shape of a lifeboat which sat on the corner of the counter.

Outside, the two captains tossed for who did what, and Ashwood elected to field. Simon was in the thick of it from the onset, dropping six easy catches in quick succession. It was as if the ball was seeking him out to humiliate him. Captain Matto, sensing the newcomer was looking a little nervy and overawed, despatched him to the farthest, uncharted reaches of the pitch, where white men had never trod, and more importantly, where balls seldom travelled, but close to where the Elder Statesmen were seated. A sheepish Simon caught Dennis's eye – the only thing he'd managed to catch thus far – and apologized for his poor performance.

'The thing is,' he explained, 'I haven't picked up a bat for years, but anyway, what I was trying to tell you earlier was that—'

'Look out!' yelled Dennis.

Simon turned away from the Elder Statesmen to face the pitch once more, just in time to head a cricket ball, which, for those not familiar with the experience, is like heading a building brick. Typically, having been sent to the uninhabited hinterland, the place where no self-respecting cricket balls venture, a beefy Barnbridge batsman had connected with a lightning delivery from Big Jim and belted it in Simon's direction with the force of an Exocet missile. Just as Simon had turned around, the ferocious ball had connected with his head, and now he was lying prostrate on the pitch without a care in the world. As he slept, a duck egg almost the size and colour of the ball itself was growing with alarming speed in the middle of his brow.

'You should have warned him a lot earlier,' said Mike.

'I wasn't looking in the sky,' explained a worried Dennis. 'I was busy listening to him talking. I only saw it at the last second. Anyway, why didn't you bloody warn him?'

'I thought you were going to,' said Mike, sipping at his brandy.

'Couldn't have hurt that much,' observed Barry. 'It was only on his head for a split second.'

A crowd was now gathered around poor Simon, who was still unconscious. The portly, bearded St John's Ambulance man was in attendance, wondering if he should stick a Band-Aid on the huge lump, or not bother. A Barnbridge player placed Simon in the recovery position in the vain hope that he'd then recover. Eventually, a few tense moments later, he did, after a fashion. He stared up at Matto with unfocussed, wild eyes and asked him, with feeble, tremulous voice, if he wanted the full English or the continental.

Thankfully, five minutes later, Simon was more or less compos mentis once more, but nursing a splitting headache. Matto's girlfriend, Karen, who would dearly have loved to watch a few minutes of uninterrupted cricket in-between hospital visits, drew the short straw to take Simon to hospital for a precautionary X-Ray, which revealed nothing more worrying than his occasional insistence that he was Napoleon Bonaparte.

Meanwhile, back at Barnbridge, the first half was drawing to a close, with Barnbridge on a respectable 158 for 9 wickets, when suddenly a claxon, mounted on the pavilion roof, came alive with ear-splitting volume. Instantly, the Barnbridge players scrambled as if they were World War Two Spitfire pilots and began heading for their vehicles, leaving their cricket equipment strewn around on the grass. Matto called after the Barnbridge captain for an explanation.

'Sorry feller!' he called back breathlessly. 'Lifeboat call-out. Gotta go!'

In the clubhouse, Dennis, just returning from the lavatory, was receiving similar information from the barman, who was himself dashing for the exit.

'Nine of us work on the lifeboats,' he explained. 'It's a bugger when we get a call halfway through a game, but that's life. Looks like the game's abandoned. Sorry!'

Dennis looked ashen. 'Am I *ever* going to see a full day of bloody cricket?' he asked himself outloud, as he stood bewildered in the empty bar. His prayers were answered when one of the few Barnbridge players who wasn't a lifeboat worker walked into the room and made a suggestion.

'We've had this happen a few times recently,' he confessed. 'We can ring up the Quayside lot if you like, and ask them if they fancy a quick Twenty20 game, just so as your day isn't completely wasted.'

Dennis asked who the Quayside lot were, when they were at home. It transpired that they were a casual cricket team made up of taxi drivers and car valeters – mainly of Albanian, Bulgarian, Polish, Pakistani, Indian and Bangladeshi extraction. Admittedly, the man explained, the Eastern Europeans weren't too hot at the sport, compared to their

Asian colleagues, but they were keen and liked a game nevertheless. Dennis gathered his team together outside the pavilion and put the idea to them. After a series of complex negotiations, it was agreed that eleven of the Quaysiders who were off duty would arrive at Barnbridge at four o'clock for a two or three hour Twenty20 game. Meanwhile, those still present could help themselves to the cricketers' tea.

At ten to four, a flotilla of taxis screeched into the Barnbridge car park, leaving in its wake a huge cloud of red dust. Eleven characters emerged from the vehicles looking for all the world as if they had arrived in Dodge City to search for for the marshall that shot their grandpa. Had there been a resident honky-tonk pianist playing in the car park, he would surely have stopped playing and hidden under his piano. Hurriedly changing into their kit on the grassy bank next to the car park, they ran onto the pitch, stretching, bending, touching their toes, swinging their bats and occasionally spitting. Their captain trotted over to greet Matto and shake hands, and after a few minutes spent tossing coins and speaking to umpires the game commenced, with Ashwood batting.

Paul and Amanda Beenie, who have not been mentioned for a fair while, were sat on their foldaway chairs, coffees in hand, enjoying the sunshine, grateful that there was still a little cricket to be had, after the lifeboat debacle. It was Paul Beenie who first noticed the police car blocking the entrance to the ground, around ten minutes into the first half of the game. At first, he presumed that the policemen had parked up to watch a bit of Twenty20, prior to going about their business of making the lives of Devonshire motorists a misery, by trapping them with their mobile speed guns for doing 32 miles per hour in a clearly marked 30-miles-per-hour zone. However, when one of them produced what looked like a loudhailer from the boot of his panda car, Paul had to reconsider. He was further convinced that his initial theory had been erroneous when Amanda pointed out the twenty or so policemen who were now invading the pitch like hornets, truncheons at the ready, and the Quaysiders who were scattering to the four winds in search of exits not blocked by the boys in blue. What followed next was, it had to be said, far more entertaining than cricket could ever be. Like Pebbleton, the Barnbridge ground formed a natural amphitheatre, and sat high on the hill, Paul and Amanda were treated to a modern-day version of the Coliseum's 'Gladiators versus Slaves' Midweek Special (every Thursday afternoon, 4pm till 6pm, OAPs half-price, children free).

Taxi drivers were bashing policemen with bats, policemen were coshing car valeters with truncheons, Albanians were skidaddling in every direction, looking for gaps in the privet to leap through, whilst Bulgarians battled with beat bobbies. Ten action-packed minutes later, it was all over, and with the exception of around three players, who were allowed to take off in their taxis, the Quaysiders were all handcuffed and carted off in waiting panda cars. On the boundary rope, the Elder Statesmen sat motionless, doing a very passable impersonation of three elderly halibut, mouths wide open, their addled brains unable to comprehend what they had just witnessed.

Back in the cramped little clubhouse, a few minutes later, while the stunned Ashwood players sipped at mugs of fortifying coffee provided by the obligatory two fat ladies who had earlier prepared the cricketers' tea for them, stand-in umpire Ted Barnes addressed the room.

'Folks,' he began, 'I have to apologize for wrecking your day. The lifeboat call-out was unfortunate, so I was pleased that you were able to organize a second game at such short notice. However, you may not be aware that I am a very recently retired immigration officer, and when I saw the motley crew who turned up just now, I recognized two characters amongst them that we've been after for over a year, so it was my duty to phone the police. What I didn't realize was that *eight* of them were dodgy. I figured you could play on with two missing, but of course, you couldn't continue with just the three blokes who were here legitimately, so I've buggered up your second game as well. I can only apologize once more, and hope tomorrow's game goes smoothly.'

Gareth, sensing that the atmosphere in the room was a little hostile, stepped forward to shake the man's hand, and explain that there were no hard feelings. After all, he added, he was only doing his job, or at least, his ex-job, and a valuable one at that.

The umpire thanked Gareth for his understanding, and asked him which fish and chip shop he worked in.

That evening, it was decided that the entire squad should go on a team-building exercise, in order to restore morale after four days of chaos, with not a single game completed. It was left to Barry to telephone Michelangelo's Italian restaurant and book a table for sixteen.

Back at the Seaview Hotel, Dennis knocked on Simon Grainger's door to ask how he was. Simon opened the door with a pained smile and asked him in. The lump on his brow was big enough to have its own postcode. His wife, Jacquie, was fussing over him, insisting he bathed it with Witch Hazel, to bring out the bruise. She asked Dennis if he wanted a cup of tea, and he politely refused, explaining that the team was going out to eat at the Italian in town, which was supposed to be very good, and he needed to go and freshen up. Jacquie agreed. It was excellent, she assured him.

'So, no more cricket for you!' Dennis laughed. Simon didn't laugh, because it actually *did* hurt when he laughed. It wasn't just a saying in his case.

'No more cricket,' agreed Simon ruefully. 'But I *was* trying to explain to you, and we kept getting interrupted, that I only ever played cricket at school, and I wasn't very good even then. When I mentioned we were a cricket family earlier on – and this is why we were more than pleased to have you stay here – I meant that Jacquie here was the real cricket person, not me, but she couldn't come today because of the hotel commitments. I'm sure she'd have loved to play, wouldn't you Jacquie?'

Jacquie nodded bashfully. She was not the type to put herself forward.

'Oh, I see. Erm, no offence, Jacquie,' said Dennis, who was not, shall we say, a modern man where women playing sports was concerned. 'The thing is, the way we play, it's quite dangerous with the hard ball and everything. Take what happened to your husband today, for example. We have bowlers who can bowl at seventy or even 80 miles per hour in these league clubs. It's not like playing on the beach.'

Jacquie smiled sweetly at him.

'Oh, and my condolences for the death of your mother,' Dennis added.

'Thank you, Mr Kensington. It has been an awful week or two.'

'Jacquie played to a *very* good standard, Dennis,' explained Simon, 'but she's very modest about it.'

'Oh really, what, ladies' county?' asked Dennis. 'That is something to be proud of. Well done. Sorry if I talked down to you just now, Mrs Grainger.'

'Er, no, Dennis,' said Simon. 'Jacquie played for England actually.'

Chapter 8

The Guacamole is Off!

'I've booked Miguel's for tonight at seven-thirty,' announced Barry to the inhabitants of the TV room at the Seaview Hotel.

The touring party was scattered around the room, lounging on sofas, reading magazines or playing card games. It was 6.30pm, that awful no man's land, where it's too late to drink tea and too early to start on the alcohol, at least for the older ones. The youngsters weren't so uptight about it. Over by the television, Jay Taylor was skimming through the *Chat Break* magazine that Mike had been looking at earlier in the week. A photograph caught his eye, and he began to read the accompanying article with great interest.

'Don't you mean Michelangelo's?' asked Mike.

'Michelangelo's, Miguel's, whatever,' replied Barry.

'Yes, but which is it?' asked Mike.

'I can't remember, but here's the number I rang. I circled it in biro.'

'Jesus Christ!' sighed Mike. 'You've booked us a table at Miguel's. It's a bloody Mexican restaurant, you cretin. Pass me your phone. I'm going to ring Michelangelo's. The lads fancied an Italian tonight, so you book a bloody Mexican.'

'What's the difference?' asked Barry.

'Difference?' asked Mike, exasperated, and looking close to a stroke as he dialled the number. 'Difference? It's like asking for a pet dog and getting a bloody pot-bellied pig instead. Italian is pasta, pizzas, Chianti, candlelight, accordion player, the Trevi Fountain, Dean Martin singing 'That's Amore'. Mexican is red-hot chilli peppers, tequila, heartburn, ponchos, sombreros, cacti, bandits, three sequined turds strumming huge guitars in your earhole while you're trying to digest the indigestible food, and then a dose of the shits, you bloody stupid sod.'

A small voice inside Barry's mobile said, 'Michelangelo's Italian restaurant, how maya I helpa you?'

Mike asked if they had room for sixteen. The waiter said that if he'd phoned ten minutes earlier, yes, but now, no, as a hen night had bagged the last three tables. Mike handed back Barry's mobile and flashed him a look that was intended to maim, if not kill.

'Mexico here we come then,' he announced through gritted teeth. Mike did not enjoy hot, spicy food.

Barry, who was incredibly intuitive where atmospheres were concerned, had a feeling that he was persona non grata, and sidled off to the nearby Spar supermarket to buy a newspaper. At twenty-past seven, everyone except Jay Taylor headed out of the hotel to walk the few hundred yards to the dirty backstreet where Miguel's was situated. Jay, who had remained behind to tear out an article from *Chat Break* and stuff it into the back pocket of his Levi's, promised to catch them up. As the party vacated the building, Barry was leaving the supermarket with his newspaper, and jogged down the road to join them.

It is unwise, not to mention illegal, to drive as one chats on a mobile, and whilst certainly not illegal, the same note of caution should apply when jogging down a street while trying to read the sports pages at the back of the *Daily Mirror*. One uneven paving slab later, and Coach Barry was a dishevelled mess on the floor, clutching his big toe and whimpering, his newly acquired newspaper fluttering off in the strong coastal wind towards the harbour, in the form of fifteen separate double-page spreads.

He picked himself up and hobbled towards the players, wincing with pain as he did so. Matto looked heavenwards as he realized that yet another of Saturday's players could now be discounted. Not that he was looking forward to Barry's contribution with any enthusiasm, but when there were only a handful of men still fit and available, beggars could not be choosers.

Miguel's restaurant, it is fair to say, was not in danger of winning any Michelin stars. The only stars they would ever see were the ones that were visible in the night sky through the gaping hole in the corrugated kitchen ceiling. It may well have been fashionable to serve offal in fancy restaurants, but they served it here because it was cheap. The kitchen staff was mainly made up of students from the nearby polytechnic, who had to prove that they could pop a plastic bag into a microwave in order to secure a job. The 'food' was always so spicy that only drunks could eat it, because all their taste buds had been destroyed years ago by macho vindaloos at midnight after fifteen pints of lager. Front of house, the bright orange gloss-painted woodchip walls were festooned with cheap tourist ponchos and sombreros. Several nasty Grattan's catalogue guitars were screwed to the purple artexed ceiling, and in the middle of the room, rising out of the vile swirly-patterned grubby carpet, was a fibreglass cactus covered in cobwebs. Simpson's-In-The-Strand it was not. Mike took one look at the view that met him as he opened the creaky front door and sighed.

'Let's go down the chippy,' said Dennis brokenly.

'Nah, this'll do,' said Shaun, barging in and seating himself at the huge, specially laid out trestle table. He could have chosen any of the tables, as it happened, because they were all available. He had now made it impossible to quietly slip away and find somewhere else, because the spotty-faced eighteen-year-old geography student who doubled as a waiter was already taking his drink order. Once everyone was seated, another couple of waiters and one waitress arrived, and began to hand out plastic encapsulated menus which contained

91

photographs of the food. This, Dennis pointed out, was never a good sign. However, this was their last ever cricket tour, and accordingly, they had to do their level best to try to enjoy themselves. At one end of the table, the older folks drank beer and passed on the starters, which, on the menu, resembled roadkill, and instead settled for a bowl of stale nachos with a salsa, guacamole and sour cream dip selection. Down at the other end, the youngsters were ordering lagers and tequila chasers to go with their enchiladas, burritos, fajitas and quesadillas. The bolder ones were asking for Naga Viper chillis added to their dishes, just to prove they were man enough to take it. In a spirit of reconciliation, Jay and Beeno had been allowed lager by Mr and Mrs Beenie, as long as Beeno only had two, and Jay promised not to tell his dad when he got home.

Half an hour later, after visiting the malodorous gents' lavatory before the main courses arrived, Jay retrieved the magazine article from his back pocket, and read it through again as he sat in the cubicle. Then he returned to the restaurant holding his stomach, and explained to Beeno and Mr and Mrs Beanie that he had a touch of stomach ache, and was going to return to the hotel to get an early night. When the others got wind of this, they implored him to stay, assuring him that a few pints would sort him out, but for once, Jay could not be swayed, and he headed off into the night.

'I hope that wasn't our fault,' Paul Beenie whispered to his wife, 'letting him drink a pint of lager like that.'

Beeno, sat next to them, was doubtful. Jay had been drinking lager for years, so he knew that couldn't be the cause. Maybe, he reckoned, it was the hot, spicy food, but then again, Jay had forgone the starters, and had only nibbled on a few stale nachos. Ghastly, yes, but not enough to cause stomach ache surely! Jay had been perfectly well when he arrived at the place, and in good spirits. Something – although quite what, Beeno couldn't fathom – was going on.

Gareth Evans was far too trusting, Jay mused, as he began to search the Welshman's bedroom. Once again, he'd failed to lock the door – he was a fool to himself. Jay unzipped the huge kitbag and was met by a stench so evil that it took his breath away. The sea snot and seaweed had combined with the already existing odours of Deep Heat, stale sandwiches, sweaty socks and used box-pants, to create a truly vile new fragrance that could stun a grizzly bear at twenty paces. In fact, Jay was seriously thinking of recreating the aroma in his home laboratory and selling it, bottled, to Mounties.

The smell remained, but where was the ball of sea snot and the seaweed, he wondered? He examined the entire bedroom with forensic precision, looking on top of wardrobes, under the bed and even in the lavatory cistern, but to no avail. This meant one of two things. Either Gareth had disposed of the foul things in the nearest skip, or he'd planted them elsewhere. There was no way Jay could search everyone's luggage, so he was, to use a cricket expression, stumped. Thoroughly dejected, he made his way back to his and Beeno's bedroom, and sulked.

The following morning, the breakfast room of the Seaview Hotel was deserted, with the exception of Jay Taylor, who sat chewing on a piece of white toast with a faraway expression. It was a worry that no one had yet surfaced, as the day's game was thirty miles away and usually the room would be overflowing with cricketers by now. Even more worrying was the state of Beeno, their secret weapon. He was hidden beneath his pink nylon sheets, groaning and saying stuff about wanting to die, which was just damned silly when the sun was shining and there was so much to live for. Jay took the magazine article from his trousers and studied it once more. Could he have been wrong? It was possible, but he didn't think so. He folded the article and returned it to his back pocket. He wasn't feeling very hungry that morning. He had a lot on his mind. Leaving the table, Jay walked outside to the rear car park of the hotel, where the industrial waste bins were kept. He opened the lids and peered within. Nothing. Not even that distinctive aroma of seaweed. Gareth hadn't disposed of the flotsam and jetsam in there.

Inside the hotel, nothing was stirring, not even a mouse. Not in the corridors, the TV room, or the breakfast room, anyway. The place was like a Devonshire B&B version of the Marie Celeste. It was as if the Ashwood Cricket Club members had never existed, but behind closed bedroom doors, they did exist, even though most would have chosen not to exist, given the choice. It would have been infinitely preferable to what they were going through. It was ironic that Jay Taylor had cried off the Mexican dinner with a stomach ache, and yet he was the only person that didn't currently have one. Everyone else was now writhing around in agony, with stomachs that threatened to explode at any moment. Most cricketers will tell you that getting the runs is what gives them the biggest thrill, but not the kind of runs that these poor souls were experiencing. If they ever recovered from this, and judging by the current state of them, it was unlikely, Barry the coach was a dead man, that was for sure.

At ten o'clock, Dennis was forced to cancel the day's game. He wasn't feeling grand himself, but he'd wisely chosen not to indulge in some of the unspeakably hot stuff that the youngsters had devoured, so he was one of the walking wounded, rather than the seriously lavatory-bound, for which he was grateful. Those who had braved the extra-hot chilli peppers would probably need life-saving anal sphincter transplants and most of their bowels removed if they were to have a chance of a normal life ever again.

Saturday was therefore designated as a recuperation day, and most of the entourage remained within the four walls of their bedrooms, praying for death to relieve them of their suffering.

This left Jay Taylor to his own devices, and he filled the time by phoning home, combing the beach and nosing around in rock pools. He returned to the hotel at teatime, and was heartened to see a handful of his team mates lounging around in the TV room. Most were looking as if they had yellow jaundice or malaria, but at least they were still alive, which was a start.

Sunday's game, against nearby Middleton Pipper, a very small village just to the west of the larger Middleton Saint Katherine, was the final fixture of the tour and potentially the toughest. Dennis had done his research on the teams they were to play against, and this team played at a very respectable level for such a small village. They were currently lying second in the first division of the North Devon league, whereas Ashwood lay second from bottom of the third division in the equivalent Worcester league. This meant that Ashwood would probably get trounced, even with a full-strength team, so fielding a depleted team that was suffering with a bad dose of the shits did not bode well. Captain Matto had done his best to rally the troops, once they'd managed to crawl out of bed, with a stirring pre-battle speech reminiscent of the one King Henry V makes in the eponymous Shakespeare play – the one that begins with 'Once more unto the breach, dear friends, once more', and so forth, only Matto's version incorporated lots of stuff about doing it for Dennis.

It was vitally important to at least play a whole day's cricket and to finish the game, preferably by winning it, so they could all go home after what had been, in all honesty, a bit of a mixed week. They wanted to end their Ashwood careers on a high, after all, and not with yet another damp squib. One bit of good news was that Jackass was much improved, both mentally and physically. It seemed that having half of his arm chewed off was the wake-up call he needed. He'd even sent a note to the hotel wishing the lads well for the remaining game, but it was a bit hard to read due to being written with his left hand. It was the thought that counted though. Now all that remained was for those who could stomach it to have a quiet, light, spice-free dinner and then go to bed early. They were probably going to be like lambs to the slaughter, they realized that, but they vowed to go down fighting. All but Barry that was. His fight with the rogue paving slab had badly bruised his big toe, and he could barely hobble, let alone play cricket, he explained. No change there then, Mike whispered into his brandy glass. It was at this juncture that Dennis stepped into the TV room and played his ace card. Firstly, he imparted some excellent news. Karen had been examining Jeremy's index finger and pronounced it fit for action, so long as it was well bandaged. Jeremy was so keen to take part in the final game that he would have volunteered even if he'd been in Jackass's predicament, so a bruised, stitched together digit was certainly not going to hold him back. This news was greeted with applause and much cheering, causing the young lad to flush red with pride. Dennis then gave them the controversial news, having cleverly sugared the pill. Due to Barry's recent injury, he announced, the eleventh man for Saturday would be Grainger. The audience members, it has to be said, were less than enthused by this and made their feelings known in rowdy fashion. Once he had restored order, Dennis continued.

'Only the eleventh man is a woman this time. Please welcome Mrs Jacquie Grainger, your landlady.'

Chapter 9

Girl Power

The breakfast room of the Seaview Hotel was buzzing with excitement. Mercifully, the players had recovered after their Mexican night, probably thanks to them being finely tuned athletes, and were champing at the bit to give their all for Matto, and even more importantly, for Dennis, who lived and breathed Ashwood Cricket Club. Even the most thick-skinned and mentally negligent amongst them knew what it meant to old Dennis, and they were prepared to sweat blood to prevent a walk-over. That said, they knew they faced an uphill struggle when they perused the team sheet over their full English breakfasts. Jeremy was back, which was a bonus, but if swinging a bat proved too much for his finger, he risked an early bath. His father, Dougie, was playing, but, as has been well documented, his skills were rather basic. Kevin Potts, a useful player, was of course now just a historical footnote, and Barry was probably just as likely to contribute to a winning side off the pitch as he was on it, so that was no great loss. Simon Grainger, who had promised so much, delivered so little, and as if that wasn't bad enough, now his wife was having a go, and batting at number eleven. Pessimists argued that by the time she arrived at the crease, it would be all over anyway, but those with a sharper cricket brain knew that a good number eleven could make all the difference if things were tight.

The decision to include the hotel's landlady in their final cricket match was met with blank astonishment on Saturday night, and on Sunday morning, the reaction was no different. The lads accepted that they needed another player, but argued that they could have found a half-decent one just by scouring the local pubs for an amiable drunk and slipping the king's shilling into his scrumpy. Using a person who was not signed to the club was against the rules in league games, but on tour, playing friendly matches, no one cared a jot, so why had their demented club secretary insisted on asking Jacquie? When Matto had questioned his decision, accusing the old fellow of losing, or at least temporarily misplacing his marbles, Dennis had stood firm, and unlike most clubs, where captains chose sides, at Ashwood, it was Dennis who was responsible for that thankless task due to having once played at county level. His way was not a democratic one, but a dictatorship. He would meet up with co-selectors Mike and Barry each week, listen to what they had to say, and then do whatever he wanted, regardless. The players knew this and had reluctantly learnt to accept it. It was Dennis's road or the high road. When Dennis said Mrs Grainger was batting at eleven, Mrs Grainger was batting at eleven, end of argument. Get over it.

Dennis, for the benefit of those who don't know him well, was a dry old stick, but not completely lacking in humour.

Having become aware of Jacquie's credentials, he had changed his stance from patronizing old duffer to respectful fellow cricketer. He had played for Worcestershire for a few seasons, which in itself is a huge achievement, but in cricket, there is a pecking order, and a person who has played for England trumps everything, even if it was in the ladies' side. A proud Simon Grainger had shown Dennis his scrapbooks early on Sunday morning, as Jacquie prepared the breakfasts, and it was obvious that she had been a very skilful player indeed, especially with the bat, until her age became an issue for the selectors, and younger, fitter women took over, as is the way in sport and in BBC news-reading.

After her England career ended, she played the odd game for a local side, but then found that the hotel took up all of her time, and so she hung up her bat, thinking it was for good. She kidded herself that she could live without playing cricket, and indeed, it appeared that she could, but when a ramshackle touring side arrived at her hotel on the previous Monday, there was something about seeing the big old kitbags cluttering up her hallway and landing, and the sight of those tall, athletic-looking people in grass-stained whites and smelling of liniment, which got her pulse racing again. When her husband was asked to play with them, she stood in the kitchen, washing pots and pans and feeling quietly miffed that they hadn't chosen her instead, especially as Simon was bloody useless at the sport. Now, though, her prayers had been answered, and she saw this as fate taking charge. Thanks to the hapless Barry damaging his toe, she now had her chance – her one last hurrah, before she returned to the kitchen forever. It was her chance to be a hero once more, and maybe even steer the lads to the first and last victory of the week.

The only cloud on her horizon was her batting position, number eleven, which, for those who don't follow the sport, is reserved for those who can't bat. Number eleven is earmarked for perhaps the player who has been chosen specifically for his bowling, or fielding, or because he's the chairman's son; in other words, the one who doesn't know which end of the bat to hold. Eleven is not the position for an England opener – someone used to playing at number one or two. This was very galling to Jacquie, but deep down she understood Dennis's decision. He was conscious of allowing his Ashwood men to win fairly and squarely; not to hide behind someone of her stature, and let her do all the work. This approach, in Dennis's eyes, was tantamount to cheating, and cricketers, as we all know, do not cheat. He needed a replacement player, and was glad of Jacquie's expertise, but by placing her at eleven, he thought he had come up with the perfect compromise.

Now, however, this master tactician had two more problems to sort out before the game began. The first was, should he inform the rest of the team that Jacquie, the shy landlady of their B&B, was in fact a better cricketer than any of them. The second was a much more difficult one. There were several players at Middleton Pipper who knew Jacquie fairly well, and if she arrived with her England kitbag and her auburn ponytail flowing behind her, the opposition would instantly recognize her and be up in arms about Ashwood using a ringer in the team – something that cricket folk tend to look down on (even though most try to get away with it).

The only solution was to disguise Mrs Grainger, and level with his team about why he needed to do so, as soon as he had the chance. To this end, he then visited Karen, Matto's long-suffering girlfriend, who, to her credit, came up trumps, after a brief excursion to a nearby shop in the tired-looking backstreets of Pitbank-on-Sea.

It was around 12.30pm when the Ashwood entourage rolled into the beautifully manicured Middleton Pipper ground. The other grounds on the tour had all been idyllic in their own way, but not one was as grand as this one. The pitch, for starters, was huge – in fact, considerably larger than the village itself – and the pavilion was one of those lovely, traditional white colonial-style clapboard affairs with a grand clock tower in the centre, and an impressive set of steps leading up to the front doors. There were miles of immaculately maintained white picket fencing around the pavilion and the car park, with decorative flower tubs placed at regular intervals, and the groundsman had created a huge tartan effect on the pitch itself, which would have shamed Lord's. The grass was so beautifully mown; it seemed a pity to walk on it.

It wasn't just the ground that was impressive. The Middleton players arrived wearing white-piped blue blazers bearing the embroidered club crest on the breast pocket, set off with matching blue caps. Their whites were also expensive-looking, with embroidered badges and the name of the sponsor – Norfolk & Chance, a local solicitor's firm – emblazoned across the front. Even more intimidating, the team boasted two overseas players, one from India and one from Australia, both of whom were actually paid £350 per week to play. As the comparatively shabby and ramshackle lads from Ashwood surveyed their new surroundings, they seemed to deflate instantly. Prior to arriving at Middleton P, as it was known locally, they could be compared to an old bald tyre with a rusty nail embedded into it. Somehow, against all the odds, it had managed to remain airtight, but now, it was as if someone had yanked the nail free with a pair of pliers, and then instantly wished they hadn't.

'We are going to get seriously dicked!' sighed Adam Trent, for he was a pessimist by nature.

'Not necessarily, gentlemen,' said 'Jack' Grainger, their mysterious new signing. Jack glanced around the ground, keen to see which players he would be pitted against, trying to remember their strengths and their weaknesses from previous battles. Jack removed his Ashwood cap and ran his small, feminine fingers through his black, synthetic-looking pudding-bowl hair. He rubbed his chin in thought, removing some of his five o'clock shadow in the process.

'That chap over there is a pretty good leg spinner,' he whispered. 'He can turn it a mile on a good day, so watch out for him. The fellow with the big stomach and ginger hair is a big hitter, but he can't play spin. Hates it, so we need to get Jay on when he's batting. Chap next to him with longer hair is fast, but a bit hit-and-miss in terms of accuracy. Ugly bugger with the blond hair can knock runs but he tends to get impatient and swipes at things, especially if you wind him up. Have we got anybody who's good at sledging? Ask him where his wife gets to on Wednesdays, when she should be at the bingo, that'll rile him. The new overseas players and the others I don't know at all, I'm afraid. Remember, it's been a few years since I wielded a bat. Now if you'll excuse me, I need a pee. I hope the private cubicle is empty in the away changing room, because I'm not equipped for pissing into that trough thing that you lot use. Oh, and if you still want to wander round with your knobs hanging out, I don't mind. I don't want to cramp your style! You'll notice that I turned up already in my whites. There's no way I'm changing in front of you lot, so erase that fantasy from your dirty minds.'

'Why not, Jacquie? Sorry, Jack,' laughed Big Jim. 'It ain't as if you've got any tits to speak of!'

The other players looked askance at their fast bowler, a man who didn't seem to have the filter betwixt brain and mouth that was a standard feature in most other humans.

'Cheeky bastard,' smiled Jacquie, who, interestingly, seemed to have become far more vocal and less shy, now that she was in her cricket clothes once more. 'We sportswomen don't rate 'em, Jim. They just get in the way when you're trying to hook a ball to Cow Corner. Just as well today anyway, don't you think? I can just imagine one of that lot asking the umpire, "who's the small chap with the squeaky voice, the three-day stubble, the moptop hairdo and the breasts?"'

'I doubt they'd notice,' replied Big Jim. 'After all, that big ginger chap's got bigger tits than you and no one's said anything about him!'

After this brief team talk, the Ashwood players retired to the pavilion to change and prepare themselves. Jay and Beeno sat in the corner of the huge 'away' changing rooms, trying to stay calm. Beeno opened his kitbag to dig out his whites, and the smell hit him instantly. It was as if someone had hung a ten-week-old kipper under his nose. He fished out his clothes, and there, languishing in his helmet, was the ball of sea snot, wrapped in seaweed. Inside Jay's head, the three brightly coloured plastic cogs that passed for his brain were whirring around and overheating, so much so that he had to clutch onto a nearby shelf for support.

'The bastard!' snarled Beeno under his breath. 'I really wanted to look smart today of all days, and now I'm going to stink. I'm going to have to fumigate this bloody helmet with my Lynx deodorant, otherwise I'm likely to pass out at the crease with that on my head.'

'Frankly, I'd take my chances with the sea snot, given the choice,' said Jay, unzipping his own kitbag as he spoke. Suddenly, he froze, and for a few seconds, Beeno feared his friend might be suffering some form of stroke. He glanced down into his friend's bag, and immediately saw what had caused Jay's distress. A large white dinner plate was lying upturned on top of his whites, and it was fairly obvious that the plate was not empty when it was placed there. Jay gingerly removed the offending item, to reveal a disgusting, congealed roast dinner, consisting of pork, stuffing, carrots, new potatoes, broccoli, peas and lashings of gravy. His smart, freshly laundered whites (courtesy of the saintly Jacquie) were ruined.

'I think I got off light, considering,' said Beeno. 'I'm going to chuck this lot in the bins at the back of the clubhouse. I've had enough of this retaliation malarkey. He's won. I admit it. I don't want this to bloody escalate, otherwise, next time he might feed my new shirt through his office shredder or something.'

'Don't do that!' whispered Jay. Give it to me. Drop it in my bag. It can't get much more disgusting now can it?'

'What? Are you planning another attack? If you do that, he'll come gunning for me as well.'

'He won't,' smiled Jay. 'Trust me. Now I need to ask around to see if anyone has a spare top. Otherwise, I'll get a reputation as one hell of a messy eater.'

At the other end of the changing room, Gareth observed their plight with glee. The Welsh had proved far too tough for the Romans to conquer, nearly 2,000 years earlier, and he was damned if a pair of seventeen-year-old upstarts were going to get the better of him on a cricket tour.

At 1.30pm, the two captains stood in the centre and tossed a coin, which resulted in Middleton P electing to bat. Matto asked Beeno and Big Jim to bowl first, which they did to the best of their ability. Sadly, however, the difference in class began to show, and in no time at all, the Middleton batsmen had amassed 85 runs without loss.

Sat on the boundary, the Elder Statesmen were fretting about ending the tour with a thrashing. Mike became so nervous that he couldn't watch, and began to read the quiz page of his newspaper instead.

'Although I may have eyes, I cannot see,' he suddenly read out aloud, seemingly apropos of nothing. 'At one time there was a lack of me in Ireland, and people starved to death. What am I?'

'Mmmm!' said Dennis.

'Mmmm!' said Barry.

'Try this one,' suggested Mike. 'An electric train passes through the Cotswolds with a strong wind blowing from the west to the east. In which direction does the steam from the train travel?'

'Do we have to go through every one of those questions?' asked Dennis tetchily. 'I'm trying to watch the cricket, even if it does make painful viewing.'

'Stevie Wonder!' piped up Barry, excitedly. 'It's Stevie Wonder.'

'What's bloody Stevie Wonder? The direction of the steam?'

'No, I'm on about the other one you asked us,' explained Barry, looking pleased with himself.

Back on the pitch, the Middleton openers were now on 103 between them, and nothing that either Big Jim or Beeno threw at them seemed to pose a threat. Matto tweaked his bowling attack, this time trying out Adam Trent instead of Big Jim. This turned out to be a big mistake. Now the batsmen began to score even more freely, and unless something was done to stop them, and quickly, they would soon have an unassailable lead. Matto chewed his already miniscule fingernails and asked Jay or and the enigmatic new signing, Jack Grainger, to bowl spin. Jack had explained earlier that he was a passable spinner, but that his real strength was batting. At this juncture, Matto seemed to be devoid of any other options, having inherited a batting-heavy side, and beggars, as he often pointed out, could not be choosers. Jay began promisingly, as most decent spinners do until the novelty wears off. Suddenly, the free-scoring openers became very cautious, electing to play defensively until they had worked out this slow-bowling newcomer's methods. A much-needed maiden over later, and it was Ashwood's small, wiry second spinner's turn to arrive at the crease, and he instantly became the object of unwanted close scrutiny from the Middleton batsmen – especially the non-striking batsman nearest to him. He eyed Jack up and down, and didn't seem to know what to make of him. Maybe it was the bowler's slender physique that caught his eye, or the shiny, almost nylon-like quality of his pitch-black, 1960s Beatle-style hair. Perhaps it was the steely-blue five o'clock shadow that fascinated him, with the sizeable section under his chin that was missing, presumably due to some kind of scalding accident as a child. It was difficult to say, but whatever it was, the young man was certainly charismatic, and perhaps this intense interest in the bowler's physical appearance was the reason that the batsman facing Jack's first ball was clean bowled. Whoops of delight rang out from the field of play, emanating from an Ashwood team thrilled and relieved to have at last made a breakthrough. The batsman stormed off back to the pavilion, throwing his bat at a nearby flowerpot, whilst Ashwood players ran from all corners of the pitch to congratulate and hug their bowler, being extra careful not to accidentally hug the parts that were out of bounds. Big

Jim, forgetting himself for a moment, ruffled Jack's hair, displacing his wig. Thankfully, the huddle of players surrounding him ensured that no one else on the pitch noticed. Play recommenced, once the number three batsman had been applauded to the crease, and to the fielders' delight, Jack bagged himself a wicket maiden. Not bad for someone who didn't count themselves as a bowler. Next it was Jay's turn to shine, taking two wickets in two overs, which saw the score reach 155 for 3.

By the end of the first half, Middleton had amassed a score of 297 for 8 wickets, with Jay and Jack taking three each and Beeno taking the final two in his second stint. There were three catches taken – two by new 'boy', Jack, and one spectacular diving catch by Matto in the slips. This was a hell of a total, and would take a lot of beating, but at least Ashwood hadn't been annihilated.

After a very lavish tea, Ashwood opened the batting with Matto and Gareth, who must have been thinking to themselves that going over the top at the Somme might have been less stressful. A barrage of vicious, bodyline-style deliveries left them black and blue, and wishing they'd taken up badminton instead. They bravely held out as long as they could, but once Matto had succumbed for 34 hard-earned runs, Gareth was quick to follow, with just 19.

Next in were Beeno and Ollie, and they too were treated to a hail of rubber bullets from the Indian overseas player. The game may have been dubbed a 'Friendly' but from their perspective, there was nothing overly friendly about it. The sledging, too, was getting a little intense, for Middleton was a team that *hated* to lose. They had even been known to rant at their captain if he lost the toss; they were that intense.

Both lads batted bravely, but when an 80-miles-per-hour delivery rattles a player's helmet four or five times within the space of a few overs, it tends to addle the brain within it, and after adding a partnership total of just 46, their lowest for the entire season, they were both out within minutes of each other, giving way to Big Jim and little Jeremy. Jeremy lasted precisely three minutes and scored 2 runs, thanks to his battered finger, and Jim somehow managed to last half an hour longer and notch up a respectable 36. Jim was joined by Jay Taylor, who sadly had not managed to find a spare shirt. It was then that the sledging began in earnest. The lippy Australian bowler informed his fielders that the new batsman had shit himself at the thought of facing his lightning deliveries. Jay, who was petrified of fast bowlers, smiled a sickly smile and took his guard at the crease, desperately hoping that the wicket keeper hadn't noticed how uncannily accurate the bowler's comments had been. Luckily, his box-pants had kept their unspeakable secret well.

In spite of his nerves, somehow Jay managed to score 20 runs before a delivery he never even saw demolished his stumps. Now things were getting desperate. Out on the boundary, Mike had buried his head in the newspaper again, reading the same line over and over, whereas Dennis had simply closed his eyes behind his Ray-Bans in an attempt to blot it all out. Barry, who couldn't stand to be seated when he got agitated, suggested a walk around the pitch to ease the tension. Mike folded his paper and joined him, while Dennis elected to remain stoically at his post.

110

Jay Taylor, his job done for the day, headed back to the changing rooms to rid himself of his pads, gloves, helmet, and of course, his filthy food-stained shirt. There was no one else in the room, so he checked his kitbag to make sure the sea snot was still there – not that anyone would want to steal it. Unless, of course, they knew what it was.

He took the folded magazine article from his jeans and read it yet again, just to make sure he hadn't imagined it.

A dog walker who spotted a smelly black and yellow rock on a Morecambe beach was celebrating yesterday at his modest £145,000 home in Preston. Ken Woolley said his bull-terrier dog, Tyson, had found the 6lb lump, which could be worth up to £100,000. Ken only realized its value after an online search revealed the substance was in fact ambergris, an ingredient used in the manufacture of perfume. A French dealer has already offered him £45,000, but experts say the lump of ambergris, which is actually hardened intestinal slurry from a sperm whale, could be worth at least twice that much.

Jay studied the photograph of Ken holding the lump of ambergris. He glanced down at the lump of sea snot currently residing in his kitbag. They were one and the same. And Gareth had unwittingly given it back to him.

The eighth man in was Shaun, the cross-dressing wicket keeper. Shaun was a powerfully built individual and a slogger. If he were in the mood, he could knock a century, and most of the balls would be sixes – the remainder being fours. He disliked having to run between the wickets, finding it

111

demeaning and unnecessary. He took his stance, bat raised almost parallel to the floor, and glared at the incoming bowler, who was thundering down the pitch. An arm flashed and the ball rocketed towards him. The next thing Shaun heard was the clatter of stumps being yanked out of the ground and falling dishevelled onto the parched earth. Shaun was out for a duck.

Adam Trent was now partnering Dougie, and neither of them was a batsman, but, against all the odds, they soldiered on to make a further 41 runs, before Adam was caught and bowled by the loud Australian. The score now stood at 198 for 9 wickets, leaving new boy Jack Grainger a mountain to climb. Not only did he have to make a century to win, but one mistake from Dougie at the other end and the game was instantly lost. The atmosphere was now so unbearable that Mike and Barry had walked – or in Barry's case, limped – around the pitch ten times, greeting a mentally exhausted Dennis each time they passed him.

This, for those who are not familiar, is the trouble with cricket. It's either mind-numbingly dull or too exciting for words. There doesn't seem to be any middle ground.

A small, raven-haired Paul McCartney lookalike strode purposefully onto the pitch, swinging his bat, and doing the odd stretching exercise as he went. On the field, burly characters with mullet hairdos were laying bets on how long he'd last. The sledging, which had died down a little of late, was beginning once more.

'Good of you to join us halfway through your sex change operation,' said the Australian. 'Never mind mate, by next week you'll be the Sheila you've always wanted to be.'

'Nice hairdo, feller,' whispered the wicket keeper. 'Who cut that for you, Devon County Council?'

Jack Grainger did not reply. Not one word. He took his stance, scanned the field to memorize the fielder placings, and then stared intently at the bowler.

'Cat got your tongue, has it?' shouted the slip fielder.

There was no response whatsoever. Jack was concentrating.

The Australian screamed down the pitch and released a nasty, short ball that was intended to take Jack's pretty-boy face off. Jack hooked it for six. Back on the pavilion steps, the Ashwood players went wild.

More than a little miffed, the Australian trekked back to his run-up marker, turned, and thundered down the pitch once more. This time, the ball travelled low like a guided missile, heading for middle stump. The next thing it knew, it was being fished out of the carp lake. Livid now, the Australian bowled a ball that had physical violence written all over it. This one was cut for four. Each beautiful shot was greeted with ever-louder cheers from the Ashwood lads, who had now begun to assemble around the boundary rope to get a better view. By the end of the over, Jack had knocked an incredible 26 runs off the Australian's bowling. The other side's captain took the Australian off, much to his disgust. His burly, ginger replacement arrived for duty full of bravado and testosterone, but fared even worse than his colleague. He was hit for 28 in one catastrophic over. Jack had now amassed an incredible 54 runs, and suddenly, there was half a chance that Ashwood could win it. The Middleton captain threw his cap to the ground and stamped on it, with Oliver Hardy-style annoyance. He summoned the Indian seam bowler – the one they paid to play.

Jack could only manage a quick single from his first delivery, thanks to Dougie's running between the wickets, which was truly woeful, but typical of a bulky, beer-bellied man who thought chips were one of his five a day. The team's tactic was to keep Jack batting, and keep Dougie at the other end out of the way, but as Rabbie Burns always used to say, 'The best laid plans of mice and men aft gang agley'. It had indeed gone very agley now, because overweight, unfit Dougie, was about to face a bowler who would not have looked out of place in a top county side, as opposed to Dougie, who would not have shone in an under-eights school team.

'No heroics, Doug,' screamed the inspirational Matto from the boundary. 'Block it out!'

The ball hit Dougie's bat so hard, it rattled every bone in his body, but he'd done what he was instructed to do. Now he had to do it again and again and again. The tension in the ground was now becoming completely unbearable, for both sides. The bowlers bombarded poor Dougie with everything they had, but miraculously, a bit like Malta in World War Two, he stood firm, until Jack could relieve him of his post. Sat in his foldaway chair, Dennis had his panama hat pulled over his eyes. On the boundary, Mike and Barry were looking at their shoes. Now it was Jack's turn to face the missiles. He blocked out, he scored cheeky singles that kept his partner out of harm's way at the other end, he knocked the odd four when he could, but the pressure was now on, and he could not afford to make one single mistake. Now, every run felt like a marathon, and Dougie was not built for even the egg and spoon race, let alone the marathon. Then the Middleton captain decided to replace his seamers with spinners, just to unnerve the final two batsmen, cut down the run rate, and give his fielders a chance at a catch. The plan worked. Jack began to play defensive strokes, which decimated his previously prolific run rate, but he didn't seem to be unduly troubled until one spinning delivery caught the edge of his bat and sailed into the air. Beneath it, a fielder positioned himself for an easy catch, and suddenly, after all that hard work, the game appeared to be over. All around the pitch, eyes were covered by hands and further breathing was postponed. It was far too painful to watch, and then, miraculously, the fielder dropped it.

At most clubs, this would have resulted in his fellow fielders offering him support. There would have been the odd shout of, 'Hard luck, Tony!' (presuming his name was Tony of course), or, 'Don't worry about it, feller!', but not at competitive Middleton. Here they were screaming abuse at him for not finishing off their opponents, and one fondly imagines that the chap would be a hissing and a byword around the village for the rest of his life, a social outcast, a person that is shunned as he enters the Dog and Trumpet of a Saturday evening, and a man whose mail is dropped into the village duck pond instead of his letterbox by a still-fuming, cricketing postman.

After this hate-filled interlude, play resumed once more, and the near miss just seemed to galvanize Jack's resolve. One incident-free-over later, and it was the drinks break, and it had crossed Jack's mind to check the orange juice for Rohypnol, such was the bad atmosphere that surrounded him.

It was then that Matto – who was an educated fellow with a penchant for Shakespeare – leapt onto a sturdy picnic bench, and rallied his men with a speech intended to stiffen the sinews and summon up the blood, prior to the final chapter of this thrilling encounter.

'Once more unto the breach, dear Jack and Dougie, once more,' he screamed, 'or block your wickets with our English dead. Good yeomen, whose limbs were made in England, show us here the mettle of your pasture. Let us swear that you are worth your breeding, which I doubt not. I see you stand like greyhounds in the slips, straining for the start. The game's afoot. Follow your spirit and upon this charge, cry God for Harry, England, Ashwood and Saint George!'

Jack and Dougie returned to their creases, both raising their bats to salute their captain. Beeno, who looked very flushed and had a tear forming in his eye, turned to his friend, Jay.

'I didn't understand a bloody word of that, but for some reason it's got me choked up!'

Dennis, still sat in his chair, had his fist clenched, like a tennis player who has just won a vital point in the Wimbledon men's final.

The Middleton bowler screamed down the pitch like a jumbo jet about to take off, before blasting the ball at Jack's head. Jack hooked it for a mighty six, right out of the ground and into the country lane. A new ball was found while minions were sent to retrieve the original one. No one wanted this thriller to be interrupted by a ball hunt. The second delivery was swept for a four. Then Jack bided his time – blocking, snicking ones and twos here and there, refusing to run if it meant exposing Dougie to the bowlers. This is how the game progressed for the next nerve-wracking hour, with nails bitten to the quick, and with tense silences that would suddenly give way to riotous, rapturous applause, until the score was 296, with Jack on 98, and with one ball to go.

The batsmen asked for timeout to gather their senses, and the bowler took the opportunity to sink to his knees and pray. His colleagues gathered around him, each offering contradictory advice. In the middle of the track, Jack and Dougie tapped gloves and hugged, before slowly returning to their places, so that Jack could face the final ball.

The bowler sprinted to the crease and let fly with a beautiful delivery. Jack stepped forward, attempting to settle it well and truly with a six, and then disaster struck. Jack's stumps cascaded out of the ground and landed in disarray behind him. The Middleton players were ecstatic, leaping up and down and congratulating themselves. In terrible, tragic contrast, the Ashwood lads had sunk to their knees around the boundary rope.

Then, the umpire called, 'No ball!'

At first, no one heard him, so he began to wave his arms around and appeal for quiet. His fellow umpire did likewise.

Once they had the attention of the players, he repeated his decision.

'No ball!'

'Why not, you bloody wanker?' asked the Middleton bowler, who was incandescent with rage.

'Foot fault,' replied the umpire calmly.

'What?' said the bowler, miffed. By now, the entire fielding side had gathered around the sweaty little fellow wearing a cow gown and six jumpers, demanding answers.

'Your foot was completely over the line,' he explained patiently, for here was a man who could not be ruffled or bullied. 'No ball.'

The second umpire concurred. 'Mile over, sorry. That's one run extra to Ashwood, which means that the scores are level at 297.'

Seething, the fielders returned to their places, and the bowler to his marker. He ran at breakneck speed down the pitch but bowled a slow delivery, intended to catch Jack out. Jack snicked it behind him, but was not in a position to see if there was a run in it – not that he cared; there was nothing to lose and everything to gain by running anyway.

'Go!' screamed Dougie, and Jack did, with lightning pace. He was virtually at Dougie's crease before Dougie had even managed to venture out of it, such was the ex-England player's stamina. Dougie lumbered towards the crease that Jack had long since vacated, which seemed to him to be at least twelve miles away. Meanwhile, the large, ginger-haired Middleton fielder was bounding after the ball, egged on by the frantic screams of his peers. He bent down, picked it up cleanly and launched it at his wicket keeper. Sadly, for him at any rate, it wasn't one of his more accurate throws, and the ball sailed way over the keeper's outstretched glove and hit poor, out-of-breath Dougie square on the nose, as he galumphed towards the wicket and victory. Had this scenario been used as a question in an A-Level Maths exam, the student – presuming he was decent at maths – would have calculated that the ball, which the exam paper had informed him was travelling at approximately 30 miles per hour, would have connected with Dougie's nose (which was travelling at approximately 4 miles per hour in the other direction) at a combined speed of 34 miles per hour, or in other words, quite fast enough for a five-and-a-half-ounce leather-bound cork ball to make a person's eyes water.

Dougie sank to his knees, he knew not where, clutching his bloodied snout and groaning pitifully.

'Get up, you tosser!' screamed Matto hysterically. 'You've still got two yards to go!'

As this latest imbroglio was unravelling, one of the Middleton fielders had managed to retrieve the ball, which had been lying halfway between the two sets of stumps, and pretty much in line with them. He took aim at the set that the prostrate Scot had been heading towards and decided that he was near enough to have a pop at them himself and not involve the wicket keeper, who would have only slowed things down. He threw the ball with deadly accuracy and quite a bit of power, but at this precise juncture, Dougie was bravely staggering to his feet to resume his run, only to connect with the ball once more, this time with his occipital bone, just for a change (which for those lacking a sound knowledge of anatomy is that lumpy bit at the back of the skull where the neck is attached). Anyone who has read any Raymond Chandler will know that this was a favourite spot for gangsters to aim for with their coshes, saps or blackjacks, when endeavouring to subdue a troublesome private detective, as it can, if done expertly, render the unfortunate subject unconscious. Dougie managed to stagger another yard, and then his lights went out. He collapsed to the ground once more, his bat stretched out in front of him, miraculously, just within the safety of the crease. The umpire, who had a very good view of it all, declared that Ashwood had won by one run, and if there were ever a situation where exactly half the people in a given spot were feeling the complete polar opposite emotion to the other half, then this was it. Ashwood players leapt for joy, kissing each other with gay abandon. Jack (or should we now revert to calling her Jacquie?) was raised aloft and smothered with well-deserved affection. Others leapt on a still-prostrate Dougie, the way footballers do when the object of their devotion has scored the winning goal at Wembley in extra time. On the boundary line, Mike and Barry, who must have now completed at least fifty circuits of the pitch, hugged each other, and trotted over to Dennis to hug him. As they approached, Mike turned to his friend Barry.

'I don't believe it!' he exclaimed hoarsely, his throat still sore from all the shouting he'd been doing. 'The stupid sod has only dropped off to sleep again and missed the best bit!'

Dennis's mouth was wide open, catching flies.

'Dennis, you old bugger, we've won!' said Barry, shaking his bony shoulders.

Dennis did not respond.

'Den, we finally won a game and you missed it,' barked Mike.

This was not true. Dennis *had* managed to catch Ashwood's heroic finale. Happily, it was a few seconds after that when he passed away.

THE END

Once more unto the breach, dear friends, once more;
Or close the wall up with our English dead.
In peace there's nothing so becomes a man
As modest stillness and humility:
But when the blast of war blows in our ears,
Then imitate the action of the tiger;
Stiffen the sinews, summon up the blood,
Disguise fair nature with hard-favour'd rage;
Then lend the eye a terrible aspect;
Let pry through the portage of the head
Like the brass cannon; let the brow o'erwhelm it
As fearfully as doth a galled rock
O'erhang and jutty his confounded base,
Swill'd with the wild and wasteful ocean.
Now set the teeth and stretch the nostril wide,
Hold hard the breath and bend up every spirit
To his full height. On, on, you noblest English.
Whose blood is fet from fathers of war-proof!
Fathers that, like so many Alexanders,
Have in these parts from morn till even fought
And sheathed their swords for lack of argument:
Dishonour not your mothers; now attest
That those whom you call'd fathers did beget you.
Be copy now to men of grosser blood,
And teach them how to war. And you, good yeoman,
Whose limbs were made in England, show us here
The mettle of your pasture; let us swear
That you are worth your breeding; which I doubt not;
For there is none of you so mean and base,
That hath not noble lustre in your eyes.
I see you stand like greyhounds in the slips,
Straining upon the start. The game's afoot:
Follow your spirit, and upon this charge
Cry 'God for Harry, England, and Saint George!'

William Shakespeare

For more information, email gt@geofftristram.co.uk